The sound of him unbuckling his belt was like a gun-shot in the kitchen. Followed closely by the unmistak-able swish of his zipper lowering. They were really doing this. He was going to take her right where they'd had a bowl of spaghetti moments earlier. *How smoking hot!* A man was so impatient for her, he couldn't make it to the bedroom. She'd had fantasies about sex like this for years. The craziest place she'd ever done it to date was in the shower and even that had been only a couple of times. Brett believed in making love in the bedroom or occasionally on the sofa. Certainly not in the kitchen. "You have no idea how much I've wanted this," Jake growled. She watched in amazement as he pulled his wallet out and removed a condom from it. Apparently, every man did walk around with a rubber *just in case.*

Titles by Sydney Landon

The Danvers Series
Weekends Required
Not Planning on You
Fall for Me
Fighting for You
No Denying You
Always Loving You
Watch Over Me
The One for Me
Wishing for Us

WISHING
FOR US

A DANVERS NOVEL

SYDNEY LANDON

BERKLEY SENSATION
New York

BERKLEY SENSATION
Published by Berkley
An imprint of Penguin Random House LLC
375 Hudson Street, New York, New York 10014

Copyright © 2016 by Sydney Landon
Excerpt copyright © 2016 by Sydney Landon
Penguin Random House supports copyright. Copyright fuels creativity, encourages
diverse voices, promotes free speech, and creates a vibrant culture. Thank you for buying
an authorized edition of this book and for complying with copyright laws by not
reproducing, scanning, or distributing any part of it in any form without permission.
You are supporting writers and allowing Penguin Random House to continue to
publish books for every reader.

BERKLEY and BERKLEY SENSATION are registered trademarks and the B colophon
is a trademark of Penguin Random House LLC.

ISBN: 9780399583209

First Edition: November 2016

Printed in the United States of America
1   3   5   7   9   10   8   6   4   2

Cover art by © Tom Merton/Getty Images
Cover design by Colleen Reinhart

For Larry and Karyn Browning

Acknowledgments

As always, a special note of thanks to my agent, Jane Dystel, and my editor at Penguin, Kerry Donovan. None of this would ever be possible without you both and I appreciate all that you do.

Also, thanks to Jenny Sims for all your help.

Special thanks to Christopher Prescott.

A huge thanks to all the readers and bloggers who continue to embrace the Danvers series. It always touches my heart at how much you love the characters that I've created. Thank you for making them as much a part of your lives as I have.

To my special friends: Amanda Lanclos and Heather Waterman from Crazy Cajun Book Addicts; Catherine Crook from A Reader Lives A Thousand Lives; Shelly Lazar from Sexy Bibliophiles; Christine with Books and Beyond Fifty Shades; Marion Archer, Lorie Gullian, and Stacia from Three Girls and a Book Obsession; Shannon with Cocktails and Books; Sarah from Smut and Bon Bons; Andrea from the Bookish Babe; Jennifer from Book Bitches Blog; as well as

Tracey Quintin, Melissa Lemons, Lizabeth Scott, Chantel Pentz McKinley, Sandy Ambrose, Kim Roar, Nicole Tallman, Stefanie Eldrige-O'Toole, Tara Thomas, Lisa Salvary, Monique Harrell-Watford, and Jen Maxner.

Chapter One

The relentless pounding in her head was what finally woke Lydia Cross from a sound sleep. Her mouth felt like she had been chewing on a dirty gym sock and her eyes were glued together so tightly it took several attempts for her to pry them open. She lay in a darkened room, attempting to get her bearings. A quick glance at the clock on the bedside table had her sitting up too quickly—which turned out to be a big mistake. Her stomach immediately staged a revolt and she struggled to free herself from under the covers—then promptly smacked into a hard surface. *What the hell?* Who'd moved the wall in her bedroom? She rubbed her smarting nose and inched along with half-closed eyes until she reached a doorway. She fumbled before locating the light switch and flipped it up. The bright glare that filled the unfamiliar bathroom temporarily blinded her.

After blinking a few times, she was able to focus on her surroundings. Then it finally hit her that she was in Vegas. Her co-worker and good friend, Crystal

Webber, was getting married to Mark DeSanto in a few days and their friend Mia Gentry had insisted on throwing the bachelorette party at the Oceanix–Las Vegas. Luckily, Danvers was a big company and they were all able to find temporary replacements so they could take a few days of vacation together with no problem.

The nausea that had temporarily abated while she was hunting for the bathroom returned in full force. She barely made it to the toilet before the contents of her stomach came back up in horrifying fashion. She was doing her best to remain upright when her hair was suddenly pulled back and someone touched her back. She jerked in shock, nearly falling into the toilet, before strong hands steadied her. A masculine voice rumbled, "It's okay, little one. I've got you."

Lydia managed to shrug out of the hold long enough to spin around and look at her mystery bathroom guest. "Sweet Jesus," she exclaimed at the sight of Jacob Hay, clad only in snug boxer briefs, towering over her with concern etched on his face. She couldn't help herself—she drank him in from head to toe. Who in the world could possibly blame her for taking advantage of this screwed-up nightmare to check out the man she'd lusted after for months? In all her fantasies, though, she'd never quite imagined him in this scenario. "Wh—what are you doing here?" she asked in confusion, before belatedly realizing that she was also quite nude. She grabbed a robe off a nearby hook and fumbled to put it on.

Jacob raised an amused brow at her. "After last

night, I wouldn't have guessed that you had a shy bone in your body, gorgeous."

Oh shit, what's he talking about? Did I wrap myself around him and beg him to come to my room? "You've got three seconds to tell me what in the hell you're doing in my hotel room," she snapped. Thank God, she'd finally gotten the damn robe tied. Laying down the law was rather hard when your boobs were hanging out.

Instead of answering right away, Jacob walked calmly around her and flushed the toilet. He then moved to the sink, unwrapped a toothbrush, and filled a glass with water. He motioned her over and she cringed as she realized he was trying to get her to brush her teeth. Maybe she could pause for a moment to take care of her breath before she continued her inquisition. Lydia quickly took care of business before putting her hands on her hips. "Well?"

He looked as if he was biting back a smile. "Could we possibly take this conversation into the next room?"

She resisted the urge to childishly stomp her feet as, once again, he made her feel like an idiot. Naturally, he didn't want to stand around and chat in the room she'd just tossed her cookies in. "Oh, all right," she grumbled as she stalked past him. *Wait, I don't remember my room being this nice.*

He moved over to the bedside table and picked up the phone. Despite her glare, he calmly placed an order for coffee and Danishes from room service. Then he turned back to face her. *So hot*, she thought to herself. He studied her for long enough that she began to fidget. When he finally spoke, the deep rumble of his voice in the quiet room had her jerking. "Do you not remember anything about last night?"

Was he nuts? Would she be standing here looking like a complete train wreck if she knew what was going on? But instead of opening her mouth to unleash a sarcastic comment, she took a breath and admitted, "I have no idea. I vaguely remember going dancing at some club with Mia and Crystal." She rubbed her throbbing temple as she attempted to re-create the events of the previous evening. "Didn't Mark and some of his friends show up at some point?"

He had the look of a proud teacher as he nodded his head encouragingly. "That's right. I flew here with Mark and the Jackson brothers. We met up with you ladies sometime during your club crawl."

Images exploded in her head as jumbled memories came rushing back to her. *Dancing. The taste of his lips. Our tongues tangling. Hands touching. My new husband.* Wait, what? Lydia stared at Jacob in dawning horror before looking down at the glittering diamond on her ring finger.

Holy. Fucking. Shit.

"We got married," she whispered, then promptly staggered over to the bed and dropped down onto it.

Just the reaction every man hopes to see from his new bride, Jacob thought as he took in Lydia's shocked demeanor.

He sat down on the side of the bed and held her hand, sitting quietly with her for a couple of minutes. Then he placed a few fingers on her forehead and caressed her gently, asking, "Feeling better?" He had no idea why he was checking her for signs of a fever when he full well knew it was the alcohol and the shock that had gotten to her.

Her earlier panic seemed to have receded, leaving a look of helpless confusion in its place. "Did we really . . . get married? I'm imagining that whole thing, right?"

She looked so hopeful that he hated to burst her bubble, but he couldn't lie to her. He rubbed in what he hoped was a soothing pattern on the back of her hand as he said, "No, it actually happened. The king himself performed the ceremony."

"The king?" A helpless giggle escaped her luscious lips. "That's right . . . We were married by Elvis Presley—or at least someone loosely resembling him. God, I still remember the—'*Thank you . . . thank you very much.*'"

Jacob found himself laughing along with her. At thirty-four years old, he had just gotten married in Vegas by a terrible Elvis impersonator. And to top it off, his new bride was all but a stranger to him. Hadn't his mother preached to him and his brother about impulse control from the time they were small? Clearly he'd completely lost his mind last night. Hell, he'd known it was wrong, but when Lydia looked at him all teary eyed and—

She pulled her hand out from under his and ran it through her sexy, tousled hair. Her large green eyes locked on his, and he found himself swallowing hard. *So damn beautiful.* "I recall pieces of the evening, but not what led up to our—union. Why would we have done something like that? Do you remember anything?"

Before he could answer, there was a knock at the door. "That'll be room service." Lydia pulled the sheet up to her neck and cowered as Jacob sauntered toward the door, seemingly not the least bit concerned that he wore only a pair of very revealing underwear. Of course, what did he have to be embarrassed over? His body was chiseled perfection. Broad shoulders and a muscular chest, abs that looked like they belonged on an underwear advertisement, tapering into lean hips and a bulge between his thighs that had her mouth watering.

Hell's bells. She was married to Jacob Hay.

It was so unfair that she couldn't remember every detail of the previous night in vivid color. If there was a God, it would come back to her. She was freaked out over the state of things this morning, sure, but the real tragedy was not knowing exactly how it felt to be bedded by—

"Lydia."

Her head snapped up as she noticed the object of her drool fest standing before her with his hands on his hips. *Please, no, don't put your cock at eye level with me.*

"Are you all right? I called your name several times, but you weren't responding." He looked at her in concern, probably noticing her dilated pupils and the way her eyes were glued to his package.

Guess what, Jacob? Your new wife is a pervert.

"Um—I." She cleared her throat and tried again.

"I'm fine. Just tired, I guess." Pointing at the table across the room that now held a carafe, she quickly asked, "Could I have some coffee?" She was sure he wondered why she couldn't get it, but she needed a moment to compose herself and get her libido back under control. With that thought, she tried to sound casual as she tossed out, "If you want to get dressed first, that's okay. You must be—cold."

When he turned to stare at her questioningly, she caught sight of something she'd missed. *Because you couldn't stop looking down long enough to see anything above the waistband.* Jacob's neck and chest had scratch marks and what looked like bites all over them.

No . . . she couldn't have. She'd never been that aggressive in bed. Surely, it was from an interlude with someone else that preceded her night with him.

He followed her line of sight, and then his lips curled up into a devilish smile. His eyes blazed with heat and she felt her core clenching in response. "For such a little thing, you pack quite a punch, sweetheart."

Sweet baby Jesus. She felt her mouth opening and closing without a sound as she took in the damage she'd inflicted on him. Did she think the man was a chew toy or something? Those indentations weren't made by one little nibble. No, she'd obviously attacked his chest and nipples like a rabid dog. She was relieved that his boxer briefs outlined his dick so clearly now. At least that was proof she hadn't bitten off the sucker. She put a hand over her face before mumbling, "Stuff like this doesn't happen to me. I've never even gone down on a guy!"

She continued to toss out all of the reasons that the last twenty-four hours were unbelievable, but a hand on her leg had her pausing to look up at a more serious Jacob. "What?" she asked, strangely unnerved that he no longer looked amused by their circumstances.

Clearly it was finally dawning on him that he'd married her. The poor man was probably about to weep at his misfortune. She'd surely marked his body for life.

"You've never performed oral sex?" Jacob asked, sounding strangled.

Removing his hand, Lydia could only gawk at him. Finally, she managed to ask, "Out of everything I just said, that's what you're focused on?" *Overshare much?* Why in the world would she have blurted out something so personal to him? Granted, apparently he was her new hubby, but still . . . When he continued to stare at her, she added, "It just never came up, okay?"

Really poor choice of words, Lydia. Now she was stuttering as she went into more unnecessary explanations. "My fiancé, Brett, didn't really enjoy the whole—oral aspect and he was my one and only, so—"

"You've only had sex with one man before last night?" Jacob croaked out. Lydia gave a squeak of surprise when he flopped down on the bottom of the bed, barely missing her toes. He lay on his back, staring up at the ceiling as if it contained answers to some of the questions that must be running on a loop through his mind. She wanted to mention again that he could put some clothes on, but truthfully, a nearly nude Jacob wasn't exactly a hardship. Their conversation was becoming more and more surreal. She didn't even know him well enough to consider him a casual acquaintance. He was her man crush, and she enjoyed objectifying him anytime she caught a glimpse of him in the hallways of Danvers International, thinking that there was no harm in entertaining herself with the fantasies.

The only time she could remember actually carrying on a conversation with him was when he'd helped her in the parking garage at the office once when her car wouldn't start. Yet somehow, she'd married him last night and then gone ahead and had what was probably mind-blowing sex to top it off. *Am I upset because we're hitched or because I don't remember my night in bed with him?*

In a voice laden with sarcasm, she said, "If we could possibly step back from my sexual history for a moment, I'd like to discuss a more important matter here. You seem far more knowledgeable about last night than I am. So could you please tell me what led up to finding myself married to you this morning?"

A quick peek toward the foot of the bed showed Jacob's washboard abs rippling as he scrubbed his hands over his face. *Look away, girl, he's not really yours.* His voice was deep and gravelly when he began explaining. "You said that you remember Mark showing up last night." She nodded her head, and he continued. "Mark and I were in San Francisco. I guess when he spoke with Crystal, he decided to take a detour and visit her. I told him it was fine with me. I'd planned to get a room and crash for the night. Asher and Dylan Jackson were here on business since their family owns the Oceanix Resorts, so I ended up having a drink with them. I ran into you in the hallway outside the bathrooms."

"And you actually recognized me?" she couldn't help but ask.

"Of course," he said, sounding slightly offended. "You're not an easy woman to forget, Lydia, trust me on that." She tried her best not to melt into a warm puddle at his words. She'd have been thrilled had he just admitted that she looked vaguely familiar. "Anyway, we chatted for a few moments, and I walked you back to the table where your friends were. It was pretty late by that point and most of the ladies were in the process of leaving. Within a couple minutes, only you and I were left. So we had a few more drinks and talked. In hindsight, we probably should have switched to water, but that didn't happen."

Lydia pinched the bridge of her nose before saying, "I still don't see how we got from there to having Elvis marry us. I've had a few drinks before without marrying the first man I ran into."

She yelped as Jacob pinched her toe. "Thanks for the ego boost, sweetheart. You make it sound as if you tied the knot with the casino janitor."

"This is no time to get sensitive," she chided, although she did feel a little guilty for the unlikely possibility that she had, in fact, hurt his feelings. Her opinion wouldn't keep a man like Jacob up at night.

His hand remained on her foot, and strangely enough, he began rubbing it absentmindedly. She wondered if he was aware that he was even doing it. "You told me about your fiancé dying and how sad you were that you'd never have your happily-ever-after like Crystal and Mark."

"Oh, good Lord." Lydia sagged back against the mattress, feeling boneless in her embarrassment. Maybe the bed would swallow her up and she could end this misery now. She'd literally been crying in her beer in front of the man she fantasized about licking like a Popsicle. *Color me pathetic.* "And you what, took pity on me and decided to help me mark a big one off my bucket list?"

The hand on her foot froze as he said, "It really wasn't like that, Lydia. We really connected and got swept up in the moment together. I could see that you were still in pain, even though it's been three years since Brett died. You had a life planned with him and then it was taken away from you. Naturally, you would feel that loss keenly at an engagement party. You showed no sign of being jealous of Crystal and Mark. You were just sad that the wedding you'd planned never came to be. So even though you were joking when you asked me to marry you, I said yes. Then we took a cab a few blocks to the wedding chapel and made it official."

It was worse—so much worse—than she had even imagined. "Jacob," she began hoarsely once she could speak past the lump in her throat. "I—I don't know what to say. You didn't have to marry me last night just because you pitied me. And I can't believe I went along with it. Was I coherent when I said, 'I do'?"

She squealed in alarm when Jacob suddenly shifted to his knees, and in a blur of movement that her eyes could hardly track, he was straddling her body. He looked beyond pissed when he gritted out, "Let's get a few things straight. First off, I didn't marry you because I felt sorry for you. Get that out of your head right now. Did I feel bad that you'd lost your fiancé? Hell, yeah. I'm only human. But your strength really struck me last night, Lydia. You were so damned happy that your friend had found Mark and there wasn't a trace of pettiness behind it. You told me about sitting with Brett in his last days and doing everything short of moving mountains to make all of his last wishes come true. It was clear to me that you could have given up and walked away, but you stayed with him until the end. You're strong and selfless. So when I asked you what your dream was and you said to get married the way that you'd planned, something came over me, Lydia . . . I wanted to give it to you. It may be crazy, but I had no reservations when I gave you my name."

Lydia was riveted as she stared up at him. The truth of his words was plain to see in his body language. She'd told him everything about Brett's death; otherwise, he'd never have known all of the details that he'd so achingly replayed for her. She could feel her bottom lip tremble as tears welled in her eyes. "But we're strangers," she whispered. "Before last night, the only thing I really knew about you was that you were handy with a spare tire and worked for Mark DeSanto. And I'm sure you knew even less about me."

Jacob lowered his hand to gently trace the curve of her mouth. "I desired you from the moment you stood before me in that silky white dress in the garage, looking like the most beautiful damsel in distress I'd ever seen. I'm surprised you didn't notice what a fumbling mess I was while I was working on your car. I wanted to ask you out that day, but—well, things were so damned complicated in my life then, and I thought you deserved a man who could devote all of his attention to you."

"That hasn't been that long ago," she pointed out. "What's changed for you since then?"

He opened his mouth and then closed it again. Finally, he shrugged and said, "Maybe I just didn't want to miss my chance with you. Sooner or later, someone would come along and sweep you off your feet and I'd have kicked myself that I'd let you go without getting a shot."

She felt dazed as she considered his words. Had he really been that attracted to her from their first meeting? That would mean that he'd felt at least some of what she had after the time they'd spent together that day.

He pointed toward the bed then asked in a hesitant voice, "Do you remember anything that happened here afterward?"

Lydia felt heat rush into her cheeks. Bits and pieces of the time she'd been in his arms were steadily coming back to her. There were gaps, but the longer she was awake, the more she remembered. *Thank God.* She would likely have never gotten over forgetting her first time with Jacob. "Not all of it," she admitted. "But . . . I know you, um, were on top, then I was, and then your mouth . . . Any other times that I'm missing?"

Sounding strained, he said gruffly, "No, baby, I think that about covers it. Thank fuck." He ran an unsteady hand through his thick, dark hair. "Last night was . . . special to me. And it was going to suck if you didn't have any recollection of it."

She put a hand over his and squeezed. "I know how it felt, Jacob. I was really confused when I woke up this morning. I'm guessing both from the alcohol and a lack of sleep. But things are starting to come back to me." Her eyes darted down as she added, "You made me feel cherished. You held me as if I was someone that you cared about. I haven't had that in a long time. With the chemo and his illness, Brett was unable to— you know, so . . ."

"I understand," he said softly. He shifted to the side. Lydia was mourning the loss of their body contact when he rolled her into his arms.

She snuggled against him, loving the musky, masculine smell of his body. "What now?" She hoped he didn't detect the hint of misery in her voice. They were strangers who had married in a moment of temporary madness. The only thing to do was to have the marriage dissolved and move on.

The sad thing was, they had been together for less than a day, but she knew that she'd miss him dreadfully when he was gone. But since he'd done what he thought she needed last night, now she would be strong and return the favor by giving him his freedom without any hassle. "Can we get an annulment since we've—you know, slept together? Does a drunk Elvis wedding really count as a legal marriage?"

Jacob's chest rumbled under her ear as he laughed. She felt something press against the top of her head, but surely he wouldn't have kissed her, would he? That would be a gesture of affection, and they barely knew each other. "I don't know the particulars of a Vegas wedding, sweetheart, but it's nothing we need to worry about right now. No need to rush into anything without thinking it through."

She rolled her eyes, even though she knew he couldn't see her. "I think the ship has already sailed on the whole rushing into things, wouldn't you say?"

"Sure," he agreed easily. "Maybe what I should have said was that we don't have to make any decisions right now. We will figure things out once we get home and the dust has settled. Today, we'll fly home together and go from there."

"But I'm supposed to travel back with the girls at nine." She flipped over to look at the bedside clock then shrieked quite loudly in Jacob's ear. "Dammit! It's past that time now! Why didn't they call or come by my room? I can't believe they would just leave me here."

She was on the verge of a full freak-out when Jacob calmly announced, "You're flying home with me on Mark's plane. He and Crystal are staying an extra day, so we'll go back today and then I'll send the jet back for them. We're leaving at noon, so we have plenty of time to dress and have breakfast before the car picks us up."

I'm lying with a scantily clad Jacob Hay calmly discussing cars and jets. Someone needed to pinch her and bring her back to reality. Even as Lydia pondered how bizarre the morning had been, she couldn't help but marvel at how well she was handling it all.

It's not as if something like this had ever happened to her before. So why wasn't she having some kind of panic attack? Delayed reaction? Possibly some kind of trauma-induced shock? She thought it was more likely that she simply didn't want the dream to end. Heck, just a few days ago, she would have bet money that she'd never even enjoy a first date with Jacob. Now she was cuddled in his strong arms and it felt almost natural—as if she belonged there, which was absolutely nuts. She shifted slightly, moving her hand, and froze. Oh God, the ring. How could she have forgotten about that? Was it real? It certainly looked as if it was. And it was easily two carats, maybe more, and there were more diamonds in the matching wedding band. Extending her arm, she wiggled her finger and asked, "Where did this come from?"

He gave a lazy laugh before putting his hand next to hers. A wide silver band adorned his finger. She gasped in surprise. "It came from the same jewelry store that this one came from."

Clearing her throat, she asked, "Was it expensive? How much does a sterling silver ring cost? Can we return it all?"

"You're pretty cute when you ramble." He chuckled. "Our rings are platinum, not silver, so no, they weren't exactly cheap. As I said earlier, I don't think we should concern ourselves with anything major right now, so let's not rush out and pawn anything, okay?"

Stunned, Lydia asked, "But why would you buy something so expensive when you knew it wasn't a real wedding?"

He looked uncomfortable as she stared down at him. Finally, he shrugged and said, "We've both acknowledged that we had a bit too much to drink last night. I'm sure neither of us was thinking clearly. It obviously seemed like the right thing to do at the time."

She opened her mouth to question him further when a nearby phone began ringing. He shifted their weight until he could look at the screen on the nearby bedside table. She thought she saw him wince before he said, "I've got to take this. Why don't you go shower and dress?"

You've been dismissed.

Before she could move, he answered the call with a, "Just a second," then appeared to be waiting for her to move. She scrambled off his chest and out of the bed with all the grace of a dancing elephant. "I'll, um—just be in the bathroom."

As she was hurrying into the other room, she heard him say, "What do you need, Chris?"

Chris? That was a man's name, right? Why had he made such a point to get rid of her if he was just taking a business call or even one from his buddy? She'd had the distinct feeling it was a woman, but there had been no affection in his voice. Actually, he'd sounded cold—as if he didn't like the person on the other end of the line.

Lydia started the shower, and then dropped her robe

onto the floor. The mirror showed marks on her body as well, but Jacob had still gotten the worst of it. Hers looked more like whisker burns. Then her nipples hardened involuntarily as pieces of her night with Jacob played in her head. She had hazy recollections of his mouth on her body—and dear God, between her legs. As her clit started to throb, she wanted nothing more than to march back into the bedroom and beg him to ravish her again, this time while she was sober. It seemed like a crime that she couldn't recall every moment. When a knock sounded at the door, she jumped backward, narrowly avoiding a nasty fall. "Er—yes?" she called out. *I sound guilty, as if I'm in here thinking of sex—and him.*

"Everything okay? I thought I heard you say something." Geez, had she actually been in here moaning while thinking of last night? She needed to do some damage control—fast. "Mmm, no. I was just . . . singing in the shower." Lydia cringed at her lie. Couldn't she have come up with something better than that?

There was silence for a moment before he came back with, "What song?"

Are you kidding me? Who in the hell carried on a conversation about something so mundane through the bathroom door? It was almost as if he knew she was lying and was trying to make her squirm. "'Fight Song.'" She blurted out the last thing she could remember singing. She doubted he knew the empowerment song, but hopefully, it would satisfy his curiosity enough to get him to go away.

"Really?" he mused. "I like that one. Carry on with whatever you were doing then."

Lydia wasted no time getting in the shower and shutting the door behind her. Within a few minutes, she was finished and drying off with one of the hotel's fluffy towels. She wrapped another around her hair before dressing in her robe once again.

When she opened the door and stepped out into the room, he gave her a leisurely once-over before walking toward the bathroom. "Do you have any idea where my luggage and purse are?" she asked, looking around the room.

"Everything should be on the other side of the bed. I found your room key and grabbed your stuff while you were showering. Let me know if I missed anything."

The next few hours passed in a blur. After they had both dressed, they opted for breakfast in the restaurant downstairs while waiting for the car to pick them up for the airport. Lydia stared at the passing scenery in a daze. She could barely fathom what had occurred during her girls weekend in Vegas.

She'd assumed Jacob would be rushing her toward divorce court with embarrassing haste, but instead, he changed the subject or brushed off her concerns when she brought them up. Finally, she'd stopped trying and decided to enjoy the brief moment as a married woman. After all, in the real world, a man like Jacob Hay was about as likely to walk through her door as the Easter Bunny.

Chapter Two

"You did *what*?" Crystal gaped at her. They were in one of the luxury rooms at the Oceanix–Myrtle Beach getting ready for her wedding to Mark DeSanto in just a few hours. This was the first chance Lydia had had to tell her what had happened in Vegas. She had told herself in the hours leading up to things that her friend didn't need to be distracted by her drama on her wedding day, but the minute she started quizzing Lydia on being in Jacob's room, she'd sung like a canary. Apparently, men really did gossip as badly as women because Mark had already told Crystal that he was certain Jacob and Lydia had spent the night together. Heck, all of their work friends from Danvers had to wonder why Lydia's seat was vacant on the flight back to Myrtle Beach.

"We don't have time to discuss this now." Lydia attempted to brush off her questions. She really didn't want to talk about it in front of Crystal's sister, Ella, who had gone to check on her daughter and would probably be back at any moment.

Lydia knew that stubborn look on Crystal's face, though, and wasn't surprised when she retorted, "Oh no, you can't just toss out that you got married and then clam up. I don't care if we have to delay the wedding; I'm not leaving this room until you tell me what's going on. I mean, I knew you were with Jacob, but I assumed it was just for some . . . boom boom."

Lydia couldn't help it; she started laughing. "Boom boom? Is that code for sex?"

"Hey, I heard it on a movie the other night." Crystal giggled. "Apparently, it stuck with me. So . . . let me put it another way. I thought that you and Jacob were making hot love all night long and were flying home together the next day. Mark didn't mention anything about you getting hitched, though." She stood there with her hands on her hips. "I can't believe he knew and didn't tell me," she huffed out. "Are we already keeping secrets from each other?"

"Cool your jets, girl," Lydia advised, trying to hide her smirk at Crystal's tirade. "I have no idea what Jacob told Mark, but you know men have the whole bro-code thing going on. So if Jacob did tell Mark, then you shouldn't hold it against him. After all, I don't think you want to deprive yourselves of honeymoon nookie, right?"

Crystal grimaced. "Yeah, I forgot about that for a minute. But I'll totally kick his butt after we get home from Jamaica. Anyway, tell me what in the world happened?"

Lydia gave her friend the condensed version of everything she remembered, which was mostly all of it by this point. The alcohol might have dimmed her morning-after recollections, but since returning home, the night of her wedding had been playing in her head almost nonstop. She and Jacob had flown home a couple of mornings ago on the DeSanto jet—and she hadn't seen him since. He'd called her a few times to check in, but she hadn't seen him in person. When she'd asked him on one of the calls about their next steps, he'd again put her off, saying they should take a little time and would talk about everything soon.

So now she had a husband who existed only on paper and no clue as to how to deal with it.

Crystal's mouth hung open in shock as Lydia finished things with, "So I guess I'll see him for the first time today since he's in the wedding."

Lydia wasn't sure how she'd expected Crystal to respond, but it certainly wasn't the loud whisper, "So . . . how was he in bed? Awesome, right?"

She sagged back into the plush chair behind her and rolled her eyes. "Is that all the women at Danvers ever think of? Sex?" Lydia and Crystal had worked together in the marketing department at Danvers International for a few years. Crystal's sister also worked for Danvers, as did her husband, Declan Stone. Through Crystal and Ella, she'd made friends with a group of amazing women there. When they all got together for lunch, the conversation tended to get pretty risqué. These ladies loved their significant others, but they also admired handsome men in general, so when it came to girl talk, no one's man was off-limits. Jacob had been a regular subject of speculation ever since Mark DeSanto had opened an office in the Danvers headquarters. She'd read in a company newsletter that The DeSanto Group designed and manufactured one of the best communication service routers in the world. And when Jason Danvers had redesigned his top-of-the-line communications system, he had reached out to Mark and now most of the Danvers equipment included the DeSanto routers. Thanks to that continued partnership, both he and Jacob were now regular fixtures in the building and the subject of a lot of feminine admiration.

Crystal raised a brow then gave a wicked smile. "I think you already know the answer to that and need I remind you that you're usually front and center in those discussions, so don't try to act shocked now. You've wanted Jacob for a while, and it's finally happened. Don't get me wrong, I don't think anyone could have predicted how you two would get together. But it's happened." When Lydia put her hands over her face and groaned, Crystal laughed softly. "You, my friend, have never been a woman who did things halfway. You once said that you'd gladly be Jacob's baby mama, and now that might be coming true in the near future."

Lydia snorted in disbelief, but she couldn't quell the tiny shiver of delight that Crystal's words brought forth. A part of her still felt disloyal to Brett's memory by wanting Jacob, but she also knew she needed to stop living that way. Brett had made her promise to move on with her life and leave herself open to falling in love again. At the time, she'd have told him anything to give him the peace he needed. She hadn't been able to imagine ever wanting a future with another man. And for three years, she hadn't. Her heart had been frozen with grief and she hadn't so much as seriously looked twice at another man—until Jacob. He'd brought her back to life that day in the garage, and he'd also jump-started her libido.

Cobwebs had practically covered her vibrator for years. But now, she'd already had to replace the batteries twice since meeting Mr. Tall, Dark, and Smoking Hot. Realizing that Crystal was still staring at her, waiting for a response, Lydia cleared her throat and shook her head. "I don't see that happening. I mean he'll probably hit me up for a divorce before the night is over." Then a horrible thought hit her and she cringed. "Crap, what if he brings a date with him? We never even discussed whether we were exclusive. God, that would be so awkward."

Now Crystal shook her head at her words. "No, he's a nice guy. Even if your marriage isn't exactly a traditional one, he'd never bring another woman to an event you're also attending. Plus, I don't think he's really into the whole dating scene from what Mark's said." As if realizing how that sounded, Crystal gave her a look of apology.

Before Lydia could think of something to say, the door burst open and Suzy Merimon walked in. Lydia had been in awe of the beautiful redhead since the first time she'd met her. She handled special events for Danvers and was married to the oh-so-sexy Gray Merimon. "Why in the hell am I the last to know that you married hung-like-a-horse Hay? I swear I swung by the guy's room to tell Gray something and all of the men were in there congratulating Jacob on getting hitched. So I drag my hubby aside and ask what in the hell they are talking about and he says that you and Jacob have been married since Vegas. That was two days ago—and no one told me? Heck, I'd have even settled for a text message. But no, for the first time since I found out that Nick knocked up Beth, I've been blindsided. Jesus Christ, Lydia, how could you marry a guy like that and not shout it from every street corner in Myrtle Beach? I was tempted to take out an ad in the paper when Gray put a ring on it."

"I—I'm sorry," Lydia stuttered. "It all happened so fast and it's not real so I didn't think we were telling anyone. It was just one of those drunken Vegas things that people do . . . Wait, are you sure Jacob told all of the guys himself? Or did maybe Mark let it slip?" She had no idea why it mattered, but somehow, it seemed important that Jacob had the loose lips and not his friend. It was bizarre, but she wanted to know if Jacob would claim her, instead of trying to keep the news to himself.

Suzy still appeared irked that she'd been left out of the information circle, but she answered the question anyway. "Gray said that Jacob told them all together. The hubby didn't indicate that Jacob said anything about an intoxicated tying of the knot." Suzy studied Lydia for a moment, seeming to read between the lines. Her voice was softer when she added, "He looked happy and was accepting the congratulations from his friends with no sign of discomfort."

When Ella walked into the room at that moment, Lydia could tell by the look on her face that she'd heard the news as well. Good grief, what was Jacob thinking? She'd never imagined everyone finding out in this way. Truthfully, she figured she'd be divorced before telling her friends anything was ever an issue. So for the remaining time they had left before the start of the wedding, Lydia filled her friends in on what had happened after the bachelorette party and how she woke up to be Mrs. Jacob Hay.

Then the wedding planner for the Oceanix Resort who was handling everything arrived to tell them it was time. Crystal was having a fairly small wedding with Ella as her matron of honor and Lydia as her one bridesmaid. Mark would have his cousin and assistant, Denny, and his father as his best men. Crystal looked as if she would faint for a moment before Ella took her hand and gave her a quiet pep talk. Whatever she'd said calmed her sister almost immediately, and soon, the women had made their way downstairs and Ella, Lydia, and Crystal, were making their way down the aisle. When Lydia took her place at the front beside Ella, she felt the hairs on her neck prickle. Scanning the room, she saw him almost immediately—her husband. He was sitting in the front row just a short distance away. She swallowed audibly as his eyes appeared to devour her. She suddenly felt naked in the form-fitting sheath dress she wore, even though it was floor length. Instead of avoiding her, as she had feared, it was as if no one else existed in the room beyond the two of them.

Later she would be embarrassed even to admit it to herself, but she could barely remember any of her friend's ceremony. She was pretty sure that Jacob had missed most of it as well because they hadn't looked away from each other for more than a few seconds the entire time. What was going on in Jacob's head? He'd made no effort to see her at all since they had returned home; then suddenly, he was giving her the impression that he'd missed her desperately.

Shit. Another part of the wedding ceremony was passing by and she'd almost missed it. Mark was kissing his bride. Thank God she'd come out of her stare-a-thon long enough to walk back down the aisle. Was it her imagination, or had Jacob bristled when she'd walked past him on Denny's arm? Surely not. If not for what happened the last time she'd indulged in alcohol, she'd be damn tempted to power walk to the open bar and request a glass and a bottle. She couldn't, though. Knowing her luck, she'd wake up pregnant this time.

The wedding party stayed behind the other guests for almost an hour for the photographer to take pictures. Strangely enough, Jacob also remained. Why hadn't he gone to the reception as everyone else had? Was he waiting to accompany her? No, that couldn't be it. They weren't really a couple. But it was possible that he wanted to speak with her about how to handle the questions they would inevitably encounter. She'd have a hard time not pointing out that they could have avoided that had he not felt the need to tell all of his friends about the wedding. Even if a small part of her was secretly thrilled that he'd claimed her in front of the people who were important to him instead of laughing the whole thing off as some mistake.

They had just been given the all clear to leave for the reception when she felt a hand at her elbow. She looked over her shoulder to see the man who'd mesmerized her all evening standing so close that she was instantly drunk on his cologne. *Dear God, he smells yummy.* "Ready to walk next door?" he asked in his deep voice.

Ready to walk off a cliff if you say the word. "Um, sure," she said shrilly then did her best to tone it down. Dammit, she needed to stop acting like such a freak around him. When he dropped his hand to her lower back, she almost lost her composure. Something about that gesture always seemed so intimate. A small voice inside her head piped up: *well, he is your husband.*

They were almost at the double doors leading to the reception when he abruptly stopped in his tracks and ushered her into an empty room off to the side. He gave her a sheepish look before removing his hand from her back and sticking both of them in his pockets. The material of his tuxedo stretched tightly across the broad expanse of his chest and Lydia was having a difficult time not gawking at the handsome picture he made. Jacob Hay was gorgeous in a suit, but he was devastating in a tuxedo. She would bet money that it had been custom made for him. The fit was too exact.

"So . . ." he began, still looking uncomfortable. "I wanted to let you know that I've told some people about our marriage. We never really talked about how we would deal with that." He reached out to touch her arm, and she felt a jolt straight to her core. When had she turned into such a sexual being? The nerve endings that had been in limbo for three years were firing on all cylinders now. "I hope you're not upset with me over it. I mean I couldn't lie to Mark when he asked me about Vegas, and it seemed wrong to keep it from the rest of my friends as well. Have you told anyone?"

Lydia was all but speechless. Had she entered into the twilight zone? It was almost as if they'd snuck off to Vegas to get married and were now discussing letting everyone in on their secret. Was she the only one who remembered that she'd gotten plastered and woke up as Mrs. Jacob Hay? "Er . . . Jacob—"

He squeezed her arm, grinning at her disarmingly. "My family calls me Jake, and I'd like it if you did as well. Growing up, I knew I was in trouble if my mom called me Jacob."

Holy shit, the name "Jake" was even sexier than Jacob. She was damn nearing purring when she said, "Okay, Jake, got it." *Did that mean he thinks of me as his family as well? Dangerous ground, don't even go there, Lydia.* "To answer your question, I did tell Crystal because she's my best friend and I figured Mark already knew. Then Suzy Merimon let me know that she'd found out from Gray and then Ella . . . Well, you get the picture. Any man you told has already shared the news with his significant other if he has one. If not, he's probably already called his mother, father, and his priest."

Jake chuckled, causing goose bumps to break out on her arms. She desperately hoped he didn't notice. "Obviously, the men are worse gossips than I'd imagined. But it's not a problem for you, right?" Why did he have to give her that puppy dog look? There was no way she could say anything other than, "It's fine, really. After all, it would have been difficult to keep something like that from everyone."

He visibly relaxed. "That's good. I was a bit worried after I'd already done it." He surprised her further by pulling her into a light hug and dropping a quick kiss onto the top of her head. "It's good to see you again, by the way. I'm sorry it didn't happen sooner, but I was dealing with a . . . family emergency."

Pulling back, Lydia searched his face. "Is everything all right?" she asked in concern. She didn't know anything about his family dynamic, but she hoped that no one had been seriously hurt.

He glanced away from her, once again looking uncomfortable. "All is well," he finally responded then immediately changed the subject. "I'm starving, how about you? The food at the Oceanix is unbelievable, so let's go enjoy it." Before Lydia could say another word, he'd whisked them from their quiet hiding place and into a very crowded ballroom. In what seemed like a strange twist of fate, but was probably Crystal's doing, Lydia was seated with Jake and the rest of their friends at a table near the front of the room. He pulled her chair out when they reached it, then slid it back into position when she was seated before taking his own and settling in next to her.

Mark and Crystal were at the end of the table surrounded by their parents. Lydia could tell by the
strained look on her friend's face that her normally
difficult mother was up to her usual shenanigans
tonight. Both Crystal and Ella had hoped that their
normally overbearing mother was turning over a new
leaf, but if their pained expressions were any indication, that hadn't exactly happened yet. Her attention
was brought back to Jake as his mouthwatering plate
containing prime rib and herbed fingerling potatoes
was placed in front of him. She was close to begging
for a bite when her meal arrived as well and saved her
the embarrassment. Later, she would probably cringe
at how she'd attacked her food as if she hadn't eaten
in a month, but at that moment it looked too good to
pretend that she wasn't starving.

Some women might be too embarrassed to show
their love of food in front of such a hot guy, but she
honestly didn't care. If the fact she didn't survive on a
diet of lettuce turned him off, then she'd have to live
with it. Her eyes practically rolled back in her head as
the tender meat literally melted in her mouth.
"Mmmm, this is so delicious," she moaned as the fla-
vors exploded onto her tongue.

She'd taken a few more bites before she glanced at
Jake, only to find him fixated on her mouth. *I should
have worn a bib,* she thought ruefully. Surely, something
was on her chin. She casually picked the napkin up
from her lap and dabbed her face, hoping she'd taken
care of whatever Jake was so focused on. When he
continued to stare, she dropped her napkin and asked,

"Could you point out whatever you're gawking at? Apparently, I missed it."

He appeared confused by her words. "I was looking at you because you're beautiful and I've never seen a woman eat with such passion before."

Suddenly, the food that she had been enjoying felt like a lead weight in her stomach. She couldn't believe it. He was repulsed by the fact that she was wolfing her food down. Why had he bothered to compliment her looks, though? "This is the first meal I've had today," she said defensively.

"Lydia, you shouldn't go so long without eating. You'll make yourself sick," he said gently. "Finish up and we'll have some dessert." Now Lydia was puzzled. Had she misunderstood what he was saying? He appeared downright thrilled when she picked her fork up again and continued. So maybe she'd overreacted. *That's what happens when you marry a man you don't know.*

The rest of the evening passed in a blur. Jake rarely left her side and seemed intent on playing the part of the doting new husband. A few moments before the reception ended, she found herself surrounded by Claire Danvers, who was married to Jason Danvers, the CEO of Danvers International, and Suzy, who'd already cornered her earlier. Ava Powers and Emma Davis quickly joined them. Ava also worked for the company, and she was married to Mac, who handled security there. Emma was engaged to Ava's brother, Brant Stone. Lydia could barely work all of the connections out in her head and was constantly asking Crystal to clarify them for her.

Emma wasted little time in blurting out, "Oh, my God, you're married to Jake! That man has one of the best asses I've ever laid eyes on."

"Who the heck is Jake?" Claire asked as she looked around the group.

Emma shrugged. "Brant calls him Jake, but personally I think it suits him. It sounds all dirty sexy."

"Yeah, I like it better too." Suzy nodded. "And I agree with you, Em. I bet the man can bring on the nasty. There is no way he's strictly missionary. Hell, he probably barely remembers that position."

Lydia knew she was probably blushing like mad as her friends laughed. She was trying to formulate a reply when Mia came jogging over on her dangerously high heels. "I can't believe I missed the freaking wedding! I told Seth that we needed to fly home last night, but no, he had a last-minute meeting and assured me we'd get home in plenty of time. Well, guess what? Vegas was one big hive of thunderstorm activity and the plane was delayed for hours. For fuck's sake, look at me. I didn't even have time to go home and change clothes," she huffed out. Lydia shook her head. Mia might not be quite as well put together as she normally was, but she still looked gorgeous. "Now, someone tell me about the ceremony and anything else I missed. We managed to catch Crystal and Mark before they went off to change. Man, she set the bar for brides everywhere. Mark is one lucky bastard."

Suzy grinned and slung an arm over her mini-me. She and Mia had such similar personalities that they were almost clones of each other. "I was wondering where you were. Here's a quick catch-up for you. The ceremony was kickass, the food amazing, and your BFF over there married Jake Hay a few days ago after the bachelorette party." Raising a brow, Suzy asked, "Did I miss anything?"

Yet another round of shrieking and rapid-fire questions commenced as Mia alternated between being excited about Lydia's marriage and pissed that she was the last to know. When she'd finished lecturing Lydia for not calling her immediately, she smacked her lips dramatically and asked, "So is he as big as his suit pants would suggest? When he has that jacket unbuttoned, it looks like a monster snake lives in the front of those trousers."

"He does have the Jon Hamm cock outline going on," Suzy agreed.

"Damn, I totally saw that in *Star* Magazine." Emma nodded. "The man had like an extra arm down the leg of his shorts. They were saying something about him walking his dog, but poor thing, that has to be a workout in itself."

Claire giggled before asking, "Just to be clear, are we talking about Jon Hamm here or Jacob? Oh wait, we're calling him Jake now, right?"

"Well, we started off with Jake, but that last part was about our favorite television stud," Mia purred. "He has nothing on Lydia's Jake, though. I love Seth Jackson to pieces, but I've stared at Jake's ass until I feel as if it's permanently burned into my brain." Fanning herself, she added, "I swear, between Seth's friends and his family, I'm constantly hot and bothered. The

Jackson brothers and cousins are in a league all of their own."

Emma elbowed Lydia in the side with a big smirk on her face. "I don't believe you answered Mia's question about the size of Jake's baby maker. There's not a woman in this room who hasn't wondered the same thing at some point. He looks fucking phenomenal in that tux tonight."

Ava, who had been fairly quiet up to that point, rolled her eyes at her future sister-in-law. "You are such a pervert. It's bad enough I have to see you practically mount my brother at the office every day. Must you also know the dick size of every man who works at Danvers? I can barely keep it together in meetings because I know way too much about most of the men who attend them! Certain things about my brothers should have really remained a mystery to me. But nooo, apparently my straitlaced brother, Brant, likes to tie you up and spank you, and Declan likes to do a little mutual self-pleasuring. Then everyone wants to know what the GI Joes are packing in their cargo pants. I ignore the questions as long as I can before I finally break and say, Mac is huge, okay! He's like a freak of nature or something. Are you happy now?" As if realizing what she'd said, Ava clamped a hand over her mouth and her face flooded with color. "Oh shit, I can't believe I said all of that."

Suzy and Mia started clapping wildly while Emma cuffed Ava on the shoulder and made a clicking sound with her tongue. "You have been paying attention, after all, haven't you? I could have sworn you were blocking me out during our girl chats, but you wild woman, you were not only listening—hell, you were also taking notes. I'm so flipping proud of you!"

The other quiet woman in the group, Claire, surprised them next by adding, "Wow, Mac is a big boy, huh? I'm not surprised in the least. I'll deny it with my dying breath if anyone mentions it to Jason, but Mac just has the walk."

Nodding her agreement, Suzy said, "You got that right, sister. If you ladies don't believe me, then watch our guys walking at the office one day and you'll see how they're practically bowlegged. One of the saddest days for me was when I saw the new hunk they hired in advertising walk with his knees almost rubbing together."

"I noticed the same thing," Mia agreed. "I knew immediately he was packing no more than four or five inches. Such a damn shame."

"But what about the saying that it's not the size, but what you do with it?" Lydia pointed out, feeling as if she needed to defend the small guys of the world.

"Bullshit," Emma coughed out. "A big dick just gets you from point A to point B faster and with more fireworks. I don't need a man down there trying to eat me to China and back because he can't get me off any other way."

When a throat cleared behind her, Lydia jumped back a few steps, colliding with a hard wall. "Didn't mean to scare you, babe," Jake drawled in her ear. She looked over her shoulder to see his eyes were full of mirth. There was no doubt in her mind that he'd at least heard Emma's last comment, if not more. "Ladies," he added, greeting her now gawking friends. They were staring at him as if he were the last dish on an all-you-can-eat buffet. Lydia had to give him credit for not turning tail to run. In fact, he didn't look uncomfortable in the least, which made her like him that much more. She wasn't sure he could do anything at this point that she wouldn't find attractive. Maybe she really had been without a man for too long.

Chapter Three

"I wanted to see if you were almost ready to leave? I thought we could go somewhere and talk," Jake asked intently.

"Um, sure," she blurted out quickly. *Way to sound too eager. Couldn't I have at least pretended to think about it for a moment?*

When he gave her a pleased smile and took her hand in his firm grasp, she had to bite her tongue to contain her moan of pleasure at the physical contact with him. They wished her friends a good night and Jake led her toward the nearest exit. It seemed so surreal to depart as a couple with him that she almost wilted on the spot when he pulled his keys from his pocket and the sound of the doors unlocking on a Ford truck a few feet ahead filled the air. He opened the door, and then gave her a boost onto the leather seat. The move may have taken her by surprise, but she was grateful because otherwise she would have been doing an ungraceful leap since the truck was much higher from the ground than her car. He remained at her side while she carefully tucked her dress around her legs. When she was finished, he leaned across and buckled her seatbelt. "All set?" he asked sweetly.

I could spread my naked body across the hood of your truck and you could take me right now, she thought. In reality, she replied with a simple, "I'm good. Thanks, Jake."

He walked around to the other side and settled into the driver's seat. She was embarrassed to admit that even the loud throttle of the truck turned her on. "I really appreciate you agreeing to come with me," he said as they merged into traffic. "We could go to my house, or if you're not comfortable with that, then there's a diner a few blocks down that has decent coffee."

The safe answer here is the restaurant, Lydia thought. But she wasn't hungry and caffeine was likely to keep her up all night. Plus, if she was honest, she was very curious as to where he lived. Wouldn't it be easier to talk without a bunch of strangers sitting close by? *Like you really care about that. You just want to go home with him.* "Your place is fine," she replied, trying to sound casual. Truthfully, she hadn't said those words to anyone since Brett died. *Don't go there. You're doing nothing wrong.*

When he turned off the highway on the Garden City Beach exit, she assumed he lived in one of the nearby high-rise condominium buildings. But they passed by the last ones without slowing down. Instead, they rode for a few more miles until they passed through the gates of Sea Crest Village. The houses weren't mansions like some in the area, but they were considerably out of her price range. She knew that Jake was a vice president for The DeSanto Group, and obviously, he made a good living if he was able to afford a home in this subdivision. He pulled into the driveway of a house with a stucco and stone exterior. He clicked a button on the bottom of his rearview mirror and the double garage door opened. "Home sweet home," he quipped as he cut the engine of the truck and came around to her side once again to offer assistance. When she was out of the vehicle, he took her hand and led her toward a door to the left. He unlocked it and they walked in. She blinked a few times when he flipped on the light. They were in a kitchen with tons of dark cabinets and gleaming beige granite countertops. He pointed out a barstool, saying, "If you want to have a seat, I'll get us something to drink. What would you like? I can make coffee or I have orange juice, Coke, and bottled water."

"I'll just take water," Lydia answered as she looked around the kitchen. The space was almost as big as her living room and kitchen combined. The taupe color on the walls made it appear warm and inviting. There were no pictures on the walls, nor any clutter, other than a loaf of bread on one counter.

He opened the refrigerator and got two bottles out. He put one in front of her before opening his own, then took the seat next to her. She stifled her gasp of pleasure as the side of his muscular leg rubbed against hers in the close confines of the bar area. He cleared his throat before turning sideways to face her. "Lydia, I need to explain a few things to you, and I hope that you won't be too angry with me."

When he paused, eyeing her expectantly, she murmured, "Okay . . . go ahead." She couldn't imagine what he had to say that might piss her off. Okay, sure, they had gotten married in some drunken moment of insanity, but otherwise, they didn't even know each other well.

He ran a hand through his hair, causing the scent of his shampoo to invade her nostrils. She was so busy inhaling his masculine fragrance that she jolted slightly when he began speaking again. "That night in Vegas, you weren't the only one drinking too much because you were upset. I'd had some bad news just a few hours before my flight and I wasn't in the best condition either."

Alarmed, Lydia put her hand on his arm, fearing the worst. Was he sick? "Oh no, Jake, what happened? Are you all right?"

He covered her hand with his, giving it a squeeze. Instead of removing it, though, he left his hand there as if grateful for the contact. She was stunned when he said, "I have a daughter. She's six years old, and her name is Casey."

"Wow, I had no idea," she exclaimed without thinking. "Are you married?" Rolling her eyes at her own stupidity, Lydia added, "I mean, obviously you weren't already married, or you wouldn't have married me—right?"

Wonderful. I finally land a husband only to find that I'm part of a harem.

Jake gaped at her before he managed to stutter a response. "What? No—God no, Lydia. Chris was just a one-time thing. I've never been married before. Hell, I've never had unprotected sex either, but that didn't stop Chris from getting pregnant. When she told me, I didn't believe her at first. I supported her through the pregnancy and went to the appointments, but I insisted on a paternity test when Casey was born. She's my child, and I love her more than anything in the world. I've always been involved in her life and have continued to provide for Casey financially as well. Chris hasn't worked since Casey was born."

Uneasy, Lydia glanced over her shoulder before asking, "Do they live here with you? I mean I know you said that you never married, but is this their home too?"

Shaking his head immediately, he said, "No, they've never lived with me. Casey spends the night as often as Chris will allow, but that's about it."

Confused, she asked, "Don't you have a custody agreement or something like that in place?"

Jake pinched the bridge of his nose, looking exhausted as he admitted, "No. We've never had a formal agreement through the court. I've always paid Chris well above what a court-mandated child support payment would be, and outside of occasional difficulties, she's mostly let me see Casey on a regular basis. In the last year, though, that's changed. She's been using our daughter as a bargaining chip to get what she wants, and it reached a head the day I left for Vegas."

She felt as if she was intruding on his privacy, but since he'd brought the subject up, she felt at ease enough to ask, "What does she want from you?"

Jake chuckled, although there didn't appear to be much actual amusement in the sound. "Oh no, nothing that simple, I'm afraid. She is demanding either an absurd amount of financial support or marriage. The whole thing has really shown me how vulnerable I am in regards to my parental rights where Casey is concerned. So I've filed for official joint custody. Since then, it's been nothing but threats from her. She wants to portray me as the absent, playboy father, while she's the devoted stay-at-home mother. She's filed papers requesting that she be granted sole custody, which is just her way of trying to get what she wants from me."

"Holy shit," Lydia blurted out before she could stop herself.

"Exactly," he agreed dryly. "I guess there is a certain irony in the fact that I have one woman demanding I marry her and I actually tied the knot with another on the day she had me served."

Biting her lip as she mulled over his revelation, Lydia kept coming back to one thing. "If you were so against getting married—even to keep your daughter— then what could have possibly made you agree to a quickie exchange of vows with me? I know we were both drinking and not thinking clearly, but were you really so out of it that it suddenly didn't seem so bad to be tied down?"

He swallowed audibly before getting to his feet and pacing the tiled floors. After a few passes around the area where she sat, he halted and stared right at her. "Who am I kidding? You're not just going to be angry with me; you're more than likely going to loathe me when I tell you this next part. I can't believe I did something so fucking selfish and desperate. You're right, my judgment was obviously impaired, and I'd like to think that had something to do with it, but still, I knew what I was doing for the most part and that makes me a bastard. Lydia, I—"

Dropping her head in her hands, Lydia choked out, "You married me because of Casey. You needed a stable image for the courts. And if you've already got a wife, then Chris can't keep pressuring you to marry her." His harsh inhalation told her that she'd hit the bull's-eye. She heard him moving toward her, and seconds later, his hand was on her shoulder. She flinched away from his touch. "Don't. Please go back to where you were so we can finish this conversation," she snapped as she raised her head only to glare at him. He immediately backed away, putting some much-needed space between them. "I asked you earlier why you didn't just marry Chris instead of me. At least she's not a stranger to you. And you liked her well enough to sleep with her at some point."

"You already think I'm an asshole," he grimaced, "so I might as well be completely truthful. Chris was nothing more than a casual dalliance. We never had any type of relationship outside of the bedroom. She's a good mother but, otherwise, a vile person. That's the problem, I guess, with not knowing who you're sleeping with. It's actually been surprising to me that she loves Casey so much because she's one of the most self-centered people I've ever known. If she and I ever got married, everyone, including Casey, would be miserable. Chris and I can barely be in the same room together for five minutes without arguing. She thrives on drama and strife, and I don't want to expose my daughter to any more of that than she's already seen. I've thought about it countless times since she started pressuring me but I keep coming to the same conclusion that it would have been insanity to agree to her demands. We literally hate each other. The only reason she wants to be my wife is for some misplaced obsession with wealth and social status. I know I'm likely overreacting and I won't lose Casey, but I can't stand the thought of dragging her through a court hearing and I'm afraid that Chris will go through with it just to get back at me."

Feeling her heart squeeze in self-pity, Lydia asked, "So you what, listened to my pathetic story about losing Brett and wanting to be married and had a sudden bright idea? Kind of a *kill two birds with one stone* thing?"

"Lydia, no," he said imploringly. "We were both crying in our beer or whatever we were drinking that night. You were melancholy over losing your fiancé and your dreams of a life with him, and I was upset over the situation with my daughter. I was just drunk enough to think that it sounded like the answer to both our prayers. You're a beautiful woman, and most men would jump at the chance to get close to you—me included."

Out of all the bombs he'd dropped on her so far tonight, that one was by far the most astonishing. Her heart skipped a beat at the sincerity she thought she heard in his voice. No matter how messed up this whole situation was, he seemed to genuinely find her attractive. *You're pissed at him, remember? Don't go drawing hearts with his name written in the middle.* She forced herself to take a hard line and said, "We need to speak with a lawyer about the best way to proceed with a divorce. You may think it's the answer, but I don't see our marriage doing anything but complicating matters with Chris. There is no way she's going to believe that you fell in love and tied the knot just hours after she served you with legal papers."

"That's the other thing I wanted to talk to you about," Jake began uneasily. "I know you assumed in the hotel room that we'd had sex and I didn't say anything to the contrary. But we didn't have intercourse. We can file for an annulment if that's what you want to do."

Lydia could only gape at him, opening and closing her mouth as she struggled to process his words. "I remember some of that night, Jake! You had your head between my—you know, below the belt—and I definitely had my hands on your—that area as well."

Leaning against the counter, he said, "I'm not going to lie, Lydia, we were all over each other when we got to the hotel room and it was damn hard for me to stop that night. But there is no way I could have sex with you without knowing for certain that you were one hundred percent coherent and willing. Plus, I didn't want our wedding night to be something that neither of us fully remembered because we'd had too much to drink."

Was she crazy to feel disappointed that Jake hadn't gone all the way with her? Despite how bizarre the last few days had been, she'd felt a certain happiness and satisfaction when she thought about him being inside her. Sure, she hadn't been able to recall that exact event, but she'd remembered enough to feel certain that it had been amazing. And now she was more than a little upset to discover that what she had assumed had happened actually hadn't. *Leave it to her to get married and have a wedding night that didn't include the big moment.* "Well, thanks," she grumbled before she could think better of it.

He quirked a brow as if baffled by the note of unhappiness in her voice. "At the risk of you slapping the shit out of me, can I ask you a question?"

"Sure." She waved a hand. She didn't think things could get much worse so what did it matter?

"Did you like the idea that we'd slept together that night? I don't know you that well and I may be reading you wrong, but you seem . . . let down when I thought you'd be relieved."

Please, ground, open up and devour me. Don't leave me here to answer this humiliating question. Of course, her silent prayers went unanswered and Jake stood there waiting expectantly. *Oh hell, here goes nothing.* "I wasn't exactly unhappy about finally having sex again after three years—even if I didn't recall sleeping with you. It made me feel as if I'd finally started to move on, away from the suspended state I'd been in for far too long.

"I knew the marriage wasn't real and that you'd want out as soon as possible, but still, you jarred me awake. Even with the uncertainty between us, I've felt more alive since Vegas than I have in a long time. So yeah, as insane as it may sound to you, I do feel as if a weight has been lifted off me."

And there you have it, folks. The speech that will send Jacob Hay running for his life in the opposite direction from the insane woman before him.

Instead of looking at her as if she was nuts, though, he walked to her side and pulled her from the chair and into his arms. "Christ, honey, I'm sorry." He held her so tightly, it was a struggle to breathe. "I've messed this up in every imaginable way, haven't I? I know it's a lot to ask, but please don't hate me. We might not have known each other for long, but I do care about you. You're probably the strongest woman I've ever met, and I regret screwing up my chance with you."

Lydia couldn't help it; she started laughing. Actually, it sounded more like a pained wheeze since he was still squeezing the life out of her. She twisted until he loosened his grip slightly. "It's rather amusing," she chuckled, "that you want a chance with someone you're already married to. I mean I know it's fake, but it just struck me as hilarious."

He relaxed against her, and once again, she was certain he pressed his lips against the top of her head in a quick kiss. "I couldn't care less if you laughed your ass off at me. It's better than you chasing me around this kitchen armed with a knife, which is what I was expecting."

She sagged against his chest, allowing herself the pleasure of letting him support her while she savored his masculine scent. "It's pretty bad," she finally agreed. "And I've gone from being shocked to pissed, then sad, and now I'm not sure where I am." Sighing, she asked, "Could I see a picture of your daughter?"

He pulled back, looking down at her in surprise. Then he dropped his arms from around her and removed his wallet from his pocket. He opened it and took out a picture. He looked at it for a moment, and Lydia could see how his face softened. He loved his daughter; the caring expression on his face said it all. He handed it almost reverently to her, and then said, "This was taken just a few months ago at the beginning of the school year. She was so damn excited to be starting first grade. She held my hand on the way to her classroom and told me that she was a big girl now, but she could still be my baby when she wasn't at school." Giving a wry smile, he added, "I almost lost it right there. Just the thought of her growing up and not needing me anymore is about more than I can stand."

Lydia tried to swallow past the sudden lump in her throat at his admission. What would it be like to have a son or daughter to cherish as he so clearly did Casey? Her hand shook slightly as she raised the picture because she already had a sense that what she saw there was going to change everything. She studied the little girl who was a miniature version of her daddy with his dark hair and eyes. But what really captivated her was the girl's sweet smile complete with a missing front tooth. That was all it took—she was a goner. Right there in that kitchen without ever having met Casey, she fell in love with her. And because of that and the sappy smile that still lingered on Jake's lips, Lydia shocked herself when she said, "I'd like to help you. I agree, your daughter doesn't deserve to be put through a drawn-out custody battle if it can be avoided."

Jake's mouth dropped open and he gawked at her in disbelief. "I . . . you'll—what?" he stammered, clearly thinking he'd misheard her.

She looked one more time at the picture she was clutching before handing it back to him. "Your daughter is beautiful, Jake, and I can tell how much you love her. The circumstances in which we got together are so unreal that just maybe it was fate. Since we're already married, if there's a way I can help you, I will. I can't let you lose time with your daughter."

She was shocked speechless when his eyes teared up and he made no move to hide it from her. The fact that her offer deeply moved him was readily apparent. "I don't know what to say," he finally admitted huskily. "I never dared to even hope you'd be anything other than furious with me. But here you are wanting to help me instead. I'm just . . . blown away by you, Lydia. If possible, you're even more beautiful on the inside than you are on the outside. I don't want to take advantage of you, though. I feel as if I've already done far too much of that. Say the word and I will contact my lawyer and have annulment proceedings started immediately with no ill will toward you whatsoever. Actually, I should insist upon that anyway. This is far too much to ask of you and I'm afraid—"

"Jake," she interrupted. "I want to do this so stop trying to talk me out of it. Unless you've changed your mind and want to end the marriage. If that's the case, then please say so."

"That's not it at all," he said quickly. "I'd have you moved in here tonight if it were up to me."

Lydia squared her shoulders and moved toward the door they'd come through earlier. "Then let's go. I'll keep my apartment, of course, but we can get some of my clothes tonight and anything else over the weekend." As she hurried toward Jake's truck, she had to wonder if she'd completely taken leave of her senses this time. He'd given her an engraved invitation to an annulment and she'd insisted on being his fake wife for the foreseeable future because of a little girl's smile? Even as she tried to convince herself it was selfless on her part, she knew that was a lie. For reasons that even she couldn't begin to comprehend, she longed to experience as much time with Jake as she could before this fake relationship self-combusted, even though her attraction to him scared the hell out of her. He was so damn irresistible, though. That she was willing to do something like this showed her how truly lonely she'd been without Brett.

You're in over your head here. Lydia did her best to push that negative thought aside. She was helping a friend just as anyone would—right?

Jake could hardly believe it. They had gone to Lydia's apartment, where she had packed enough outfit changes to get her through several days, along with her toiletries. He was leading her down the hallway and into his guest room now. He'd fully expected her to rip into him when he'd confessed everything from that night, and she had been angry—at first. Then she'd appeared almost despondent.

He'd wanted to see her again sooner, but Chris had been calling him and dropping by unannounced for the last two days. She insisted that if he would only agree to marry her, all of their problems could go away. He wondered if she knew just how insane that sounded. He'd finally told her the night before that he'd had enough, and surprisingly she'd actually listened and had backed off today. He knew it wouldn't last, but he was enjoying the peace while he could. If not for dealing with that since he'd been home, he would have been on Lydia's doorstep—once he actually figured out where that was.

Parts of their night together in Las Vegas were still fuzzy, but the desire he'd felt for her wasn't one of them. It had haunted him since coming home. That night, as they'd sat together in the hotel bar after their friends had left, they had bonded over their shared misery. He hadn't revealed his as she had, but it had been there, choking him. The last thing he'd been thinking when he took the seat beside her was getting into a serious relationship. Hell, he'd been trying to avoid marriage with Chris for months. But as Lydia had told him about losing her fiancé and how it had crushed her dreams of sharing her life with someone, suddenly it had been as if a lightbulb had gone off in his head. Each of them was longing to have someone special in their life. He certainly couldn't replace the fiancé she had lost, but he could give her the husband she longed for and she could be the noncrazy wife he needed for his daughter. No doubt about it, the beer goggles had truly been on and his idea had seemed absolutely perfect. The fact that he was drawn to Lydia in a way he couldn't explain hadn't hurt either.

In the sober light of the next day, he was still very attracted to her, but that was overridden by the guilt he felt at what had seemed much more like deception than friends helping each other. So the fact that she was here with him now was more than he would have thought possible. It also pushed the point home that he hadn't planned what would happen beyond their I do's. Did they live together as roommates? Split the household chores down the middle and have separate lives? Or did they attempt to form some kind of relationship—at the very least they could probably manage a friendship. If he was honest with himself, he wouldn't mind something more. He'd like to get to know her better. It'd been a while since he'd had any interest in a woman that ran deeper than a bedmate for a night. Dealing with Chris and her demands had left him quite cynical where the opposite sex was concerned. But Lydia was so different from the mother of his child.

When she touched his arm, he realized she'd been talking to him—or trying to—but he'd been too zoned out to notice. "Sorry, what was that?" he asked, feeling awkward as hell. He found himself wanting to impress her, and he sure hadn't been successful at that so far. He was the VP of a very profitable company but had all of the grace of a schoolboy around her.

Before she could answer, she let out a huge yawn and immediately blushed a pretty shade of pink.

"Sorry about that," she murmured. "I was actually asking if it was okay if I turned in for the night. It's gotten pretty late, and I was up early this morning helping Crystal."

"Oh, of course," Jake answered quickly, feeling like a heel for keeping her up. Now that she'd mentioned it, he could see the telltale signs of fatigue on her face. He deposited her suitcase inside the doorway. "The bathroom is right through there," he added, pointing it out. Then he stood with his hands in his pockets feeling a little uncertain as to what to do next.

Casey was the only overnight guest he'd had in years. When his parents were in town, they usually chose to stay at a beachside hotel, and his brother, Josh—well, he tried not to imagine where he ended up most nights when he visited.

Lydia gave him an amused smirk. "I think I can take it from here. If I have any problems, I'll let you know."

He backed away so suddenly, he stumbled, nearly falling onto his ass. *You're so smooth, I can't imagine why she wants to be rid of you.* "So . . . I'm just down the hall if you need anything. It's the first door on the right." He turned to leave and then swung back around. "Actually, that's wrong. It's the first door on the left from your room. It's the right from the living room. Or would you consider it the last door technically?"

"I'll scream," Lydia deadpanned. At his alarmed expression, she giggled before adding, "I meant if I can't find you, I'll just yell your name."

"Oh . . . right." He smiled before reluctantly walking away and shutting the door behind him. He was making such an ass out of himself that he should have cut his losses and bolted immediately instead of hanging around her room like some kind of creeper.

If what had just occurred was any indication, his pretend marriage was going to be one hell of a trip. He was usually pretty smooth around the ladies, but that certainly hadn't been the case just now. He needed to get his shit together and fast. Maybe if he and Lydia sat down again tomorrow and further defined the parameters of their relationship, he might be more comfortable around her. As it stood now, he had no idea how long she planned to remain his wife—or what exactly that relationship entailed. If they were going to live together, though, things needed to be spelled out between them so there were no misunderstandings.

Every moment he was around her, his attraction to her only grew stronger. He owed her so much for agreeing to help him with the Chris situation. He didn't want to push his luck, but damn if he didn't want to do something crazy like ask her out on a date. *Be grateful that she's still speaking to you and leave it at that tonight.* He decided to listen to the wise voice in his head and go about his usual nightly routine. One that normally didn't include having a wife just down the hall. He had no idea how he'd ever sleep, but he also suspected he should get used to the frustration because he had a feeling he hadn't seen anything yet.

When you got fake married, it likely meant other women were probably off the menu for a while.

Chapter Four

When Lydia woke up on Sunday morning, it hit her that she hadn't thought the whole moving in with Jake thing over very well. Normally, she would have spent her day doing laundry and getting prepared for the week ahead. Sometimes she would have lunch or dinner with a friend, but those get-togethers had grown rare since Crystal met Mark. Naturally, her friend was part of a couple now and spent most of her free time with her man. Lydia didn't begrudge her that; after all, she'd been that woman once when Brett was alive. Even after three years, she still had trouble adjusting to being single. She'd made joint decisions for so long that she automatically felt like she should consult someone before agreeing to anything.

Not knowing what else to do, she showered and dressed in a pair of skinny jeans and a fitted white top. She threw on a pair of low-heeled sandals and took a breath before stepping out into the hall. She was bracing herself to see Jake again when she caught a flash of motion before something slammed into her legs.

She rocked back, just barely managing to catch herself. "What the . . ." she murmured as she tried to get her bearings.

Then she heard a giggle before a childish voice asked, "Who are you?"

Lydia looked down to find Jake's daughter grinning up at her. Dear Lord, the child was more beautiful in person and resembled her daddy even more. And those dimples. Lydia could feel her insides melting into a gooey mess. She squatted down, bringing herself eye level with the curious little girl. "I'm Lydia and I believe that you're Casey."

The little girl screwed up her face before asking, "Are you a stranger? 'Cause I can't talk to you if you are." Abruptly, her small face zeroed in on Lydia's feet. "Can I wear your shoes? I like sparkles. Mommy says they make girls look like ramps, but I don't see how. My cousin, Kendall, has a ramp for his skates. But it don't look nothing like sparkly shoes. So . . . can you please take them off now?"

Before Lydia could stop her head from spinning with all of the rapid-fire words coming from Casey's mouth, the little girl had removed her own shiny black sandals and was tugging on Lydia's. "Honey, maybe we should ask your dad first," she managed to spit out. When Casey's lip wobbled and she appeared on the verge of tears, Lydia stepped out of her shoes without another word of protest. "Okay, here you go, sweetheart. Do you need me to help you put them on?"

Casey gave her a sweet smile that no longer showed any trace of tears. Lydia was pretty sure she'd been hustled by a six-year-old. The little girl plopped on her bottom and preceded to push her tiny feet into Lydia's shoes. She was grateful at least that they didn't have any type of heel that would make them dangerous for her to wear. "You've got big feet," Casey tossed out as she stood back up. Then she grabbed Lydia's hand and began tugging her down the hallway. "Let's go show Mommy my ramp shoes!" Resistance was futile at that point. Casey was hell-bent on finding her mother, and Lydia was very much afraid that she'd given Jake's daughter a pair of tramp shoes to wear. What else could "ramp" mean? She knew darn well it wasn't some skating reference.

She barely had a moment to panic before Casey had her in the kitchen standing just inches away from a tense Jake and an obviously angry but beautiful woman who had to be Chris. *Of course, the mother of his child would look like a supermodel. Should I have expected anything less?* She had the kind of flowing locks that women paid big money to achieve with hair extensions. It was also readily apparent that she spent a lot of time in a gym, no doubt with a personal trainer. Plus, her makeup was flawless and her features would have been beautiful if not for the scowl currently marring her face.

"Daddy, look what I found in your bedroom!" Casey's voice seemed to reverberate around the kitchen, causing the adults to stiffen.

Chris put her hands on her designer jean–clad hips and hissed, "For God's sake, Jake, really? You've just been standing here telling me how important it is to set a good example for *our* daughter, and you have some tramp in your bedroom the whole time?"

The word "tramp" registered with Casey almost immediately, and Lydia winced as the little girl began pointing frantically to her feet. "She let me wear her ramps, Mommy! She had them on, but now I got them." Then she wrinkled her little nose and added, "But I don't think she got skates."

Lydia knew she should be angry at the insult from Chris, but she was so horrified to be stuck in the middle of this train wreck that all she could do was stand stock-still while it played out before her. To her amazement, laughter boomed through the air and Jake bent over, holding his side. "Ramps? What the heck does that mean?"

Chris sniffed indignantly. "She's referring to the type of women you've dragged into your house. The one who is presently standing beside *my* impressionable daughter!"

Jake stood there for a moment as if doing the math in his head before her insult finally got through to him. He seemed to lose all of his mirth as his jaw hardened. "Christina, this conversation is hardly appropriate for Casey. And the fact that you've used *that* word around her before completely boggles the mind."

Lydia had no experience with parenting, but still she felt that Jake and Chris should be having this discussion elsewhere. They might not have noticed it, but their daughter was watching them with rapt attention. So Lydia squared her shoulders and cleared her throat uneasily. When she had everyone's attention, she looked at Casey pointedly before turning back to Jake and Chris. "If you don't mind, I thought I could go into the other room with Casey and watch television." *Anything loud enough to block the sound of their bickering*, she thought, but didn't verbalize it.

"Absolutely not!" Chris snapped out. The other woman might be beautiful on the outside, but the sneer on her face and the contempt in her voice made her very ugly to Lydia at that moment. She stalked over to her daughter and gritted out, "Take those shoes off, Casey. We're leaving now."

Obviously, Casey noticed the tone of her mother's voice and wisely didn't argue. Instead, she slid her small feet from Lydia's shoes, and then bent down to pick them up. "Thank you for letting me wear your ramps," she whispered politely.

"You're welcome, sweetheart," Lydia said softly, feeling anguish for the little girl. This child, like so many, didn't deserve to be caught in the war that raged between her parents. She shouldn't have to worry about anything more important than her next tea party or learning new things at school. She glanced quickly at her mother, before bolting across the room and connecting with her father's leg.

He leaned down and scooped her up into his arms. Lydia was certain she saw moisture in his eyes as he buried his face in his daughter's soft curls. "Daddy loves you, baba. I'll see you real soon, okay?"

"Must you insist on calling her that?" Chris huffed out, before stepping over to Jake and taking a reluctant Casey in her arms for a brief second before putting her on her feet. "Let's go find your shoes." The kitchen was dead silent as they each seemed to be waiting for them to either reappear or for the sound of the door closing. A few minutes later, a slam reverberated through the house and Jake slumped around the bar.

"I'm sorry, Lydia. That should have never happened in front of you or Casey. I didn't tell her about our marriage today for the very same reason. I figured I'd talk to her while Casey was at school one day this week. But she dropped by unannounced this morning in a foul mood. I tried to hold my tongue to keep it from escalating, but even that pissed her off. When you and Casey walked in the kitchen, she was looking for a reason to blow and she got it. She's angry over the joint custody papers I filed and she's in my face at every opportunity about it. I'm not sure what she hopes to gain from these impromptu visits. The only bright spot is getting to see Casey, even though it's unexpected."

Lydia walked toward him and laid a hand on his arm. "It's all right," she replied. "I shouldn't have come into the room when I knew she was here." Giving him an amused look, she added, "But your daughter doesn't take no for an answer very easily. She towed and I followed."

Jake chuckled then put his other hand over hers. She bit her lip to keep from moaning at the feel of his warm skin beneath her hand. Touching him probably hadn't been the best idea. "She is a lot like her father in that respect. I also apologize about the whole ramp-tramp thing. It's beyond my comprehension why Chris would say that in front of her. Trust me, that conversation is far from over."

Worried, Lydia asked, "Do you think us being married is really going to help your case? She seemed so . . . hostile today. I'm afraid that it will just make her worse."

Looking disgusted, he shook his head. "Oh, undoubtedly it will make Chris more of a bitch than usual. She set all of this into motion, though, with her absurd demands." When the door slammed once again, they both stared at each other in shock. "What the hell?" Jake retorted as he pulled away from her to see who their visitor was. He'd barely rounded the corner when the reappearance of his now grinning daughter brought him to an abrupt halt.

Chris was just inches behind her and looked as if she'd swallowed something sour as she rolled her eyes and said, "Can Casey stay with you for a few hours? My mother was supposed to watch her today while I helped a friend with a baby shower. But apparently, she's been up sick all night and just now saw fit to let me know." Lydia wondered idly why it would be a problem for Chris to take her daughter with her but wisely kept her mouth shut. She didn't want to risk another round of being called a tramp—or a ramp as Casey put it.

"Of course," Jake replied without hesitation. "How about I drop her by this evening around seven? We'll go to the aquarium or to the zoo."

Casey jumped in place, clearly excited by her father's plans for the day. "I want to go to the quarium,

Daddy, and pet a fish!" Lydia was smiling at the little girl, thinking about how adorable she was when Casey unknowingly threw her under the bus. She grabbed Lydia's hand and tugged on it. "Can she come with us too, Daddy?" Without waiting for Jake's reply, she told Lydia, "You gonna love those fishes. And if you lay on your tummy on the rocks, they'll let you pet the big ones. No standing up, though, 'cause you might fall in the water."

It was a testament to how much Chris wanted a babysitter that instead of making another scene, she simply settled for glaring from Jake to Lydia before saying stiffly, "I'll be expecting her at seven. I'd appreciate it if you didn't confuse her by including someone she'll never see again after today. I'd rather not answer any questions as to who Daddy's special friend is."

Lydia could see the frustration on Jake's face, and she couldn't blame him. Actually, she had to give him a lot of credit for not telling the other woman off. There was rude and then there was Chris. She seemed to be in a league all her own. Lydia had a feeling that she chose to do a lot of her taunting in front of her daughter because she realized he would be less likely to retaliate in the same manner. He blew out an exasperated breath before saying, "We'll discuss that this evening when I drop off Casey."

Chris shrugged her shoulders and whirled on her impossibly high heels. Almost like something out of a movie, her long, pale hair floated behind her as she tossed a "Whatever" over her slim shoulders.

What a bitch, Lydia couldn't help thinking as the

three of them were left behind in an obviously expensive cloud of perfume. Jake pasted on a big smile for his daughter and clapped his hands together. "All right! Who wants to see some sharks?"

"Me do, me do!" Casey whirled and bobbed before latching on to her father's leg.

Lydia stood uncertainly, not knowing if she was invited or if he wanted to spend the time alone with his daughter. How comfortable could he possibly be with her going along, seeing as they barely knew each other? He was probably too much of a gentleman to exclude her, though, so she decided to make it easy for him. "I think I'll get my clothes ready for the week ahead and then curl up with a book this afternoon. You two go ahead and have a blast."

Jake's jaw dropped at her words. "What? Why? I thought . . . I mean, don't you want to come with us? Do you not enjoy aquariums? The one at Broadway is amazing. We'll grab some lunch afterward and walk around."

She shifted uncertainly. She really did want to go, and he appeared to genuinely desire her company as well. Before she could answer, Casey took first her daddy's hand and then Lydia's. "Let's go!" she announced.

Jake gave her a playful grin over his daughter's head knowing full well that she wouldn't say no to the little girl—and she didn't. Within minutes, Casey was buckled in the backseat of Jake's truck while Lydia took her seat beside him.

"Thanks for coming along," he said as they drove

the short distance through Myrtle Beach to Broadway at the Beach. It was a mix of shops, restaurants, and attractions such as Ripley's Aquarium.

Figuring she might as well come clean, Lydia said, "No problem. I have a membership to the aquarium, so I'm there quite a lot. I've found it's a pretty good place to spend a lazy day. Plus, they're constantly adding different exhibits, so there's always something new to see." *Did that explanation make her sound like a loser?* she wondered wryly. He probably thought she had no life. How many single women spent time hanging out at a local attraction geared primarily toward children? She didn't want to add that Brett had originally gotten the membership for the two of them to enjoy together, and she hadn't had the heart to cancel it. So each year, she paid the membership fee. And on the days that she missed him the most, she would often find herself driving there and spending time doing one of the things that he'd enjoyed so much. She'd always thought that someday they'd bring their own child to learn about some of the aquatic habitats from around the world, but that hope had died along with Brett.

Lydia had been so engrossed in her thoughts that she jerked when a hand landed on her knee. "Is everything okay?" Jake asked, sounding concerned. It was then that she realized tears were trailing down her cheeks.

"Oh God," she squeaked out as she quickly wiped away the moisture.

"Hang on, honey, let me find somewhere to pull over," he said as he slowed the truck.

"No, Jake," she rushed out. "Please—I'm fine."
When he continued to throw uncertain looks her way,
she sighed before saying, "I used to go to the aquarium
with Brett. He loved it and I've kept the membership
all these years because it held many good memories
for me. I realize that may sound silly to you, but—"

"Why would it?" Jake interrupted. "Of course you
would feel that way about any place you and he fre-
quented together. Heck, I get a stupid grin on my face
when I go in McDonald's because I'll recall something
silly that Casey did on the playground when we were
there together the last time. There is no right or wrong
in how we feel—it just is. That said, if going here is
going to be too hard for you, we'll go somewhere else.
And it won't be any kind of inconvenience." He'd continued to hold her leg, but now his fingers were idly
caressing the sensitive skin of her inner thigh as well.
She didn't think he was even aware he was doing it,
but she certainly was. She'd gone from sobbing over
Brett to one big mass of quivering awareness at the
touch of another man. If she was ever to move on with
her life, then she needed to stop feeling so conflicted
and just enjoy Jake's comfort and his touch.

She dropped her hand over his for the second time
that day and squeezed. "I'd really like to share it with
you and Casey."

He surprised her by shifting his hand under hers
until their fingers entwined. He kept his eyes on the
road but said softly, "We'd like that too, sweetheart."

No matter how hard she tried to tell herself not to
be swept away in all things Jake, her heart still

thudded heavily in her chest when he made no move to pull away. He continued to surprise her—in mostly good ways. It was obvious to anyone with eyes that he was drop-dead handsome and oh so sexy. She'd even suspected he was a good guy after he came to her rescue in the parking garage that day. Most men would have been terrified to deal with a crying woman, but he'd actually been very sweet and thoughtful. Some lady was going to be very lucky when he decided to settle down for real.

Their marriage had been on borrowed time from the moment they said, "I do." If she was already attached after one day, how would she possibly deal with the aftermath of losing something she never really had?

Jacob stood watching his daughter and Lydia as they lay on their stomachs to pet the stingrays in the aquarium bay. To say these two had become fast friends was an understatement. Casey had practically hung on Lydia's every word as they moved through each exhibit. Lydia told Casey fun facts about each fish in a way that she could understand, and he'd been about as captivated as his daughter by the time they were nearing the last areas. Whether she knew it or not, Lydia seemed born to be a mother. She was nurturing in a way that Chris had never been. She might love their daughter, but she'd never be the soccer mom who brought cupcakes to the matches or invited the other kids over for a slumber party. The only way Chris would entertain another child was if it was socially advantageous to do so. She had no qualms about using Casey as a stepping-stone to make connections with well-to-do parents.

Casey shrieked in pure delight when her hand touched one of the rays as it passed by. "Lydie, did you see? I feels its whole back!"

Lydia threw her arm around his daughter and squeezed her. "I did! That was awesome. How long are your arms, little miss? I stretched as far as I could and I still missed it!"

Jacob's chest felt unusually tight as Casey beamed up at Lydia before turning to look at him. "It's okay, Lydie. Daddy'll let us wait til you gets one. Right, Daddy?"

"Of course I will, baba," he choked out, feeling strangely moved by seeing the woman who was technically his wife interact with his child. How he wished for Casey's sake that she could have a woman this nurturing in her life all the time. Chris might love her, but she was as different as night and day from Lydia.

They ended up staying at the stingray exhibit for another thirty minutes until Casey was ready to move on to the gift shop at the end of the tour. Then Casey jumped up from her position at the bay and skipped past him to look at the stuffed animals a few feet away. He walked forward and extended a hand to help a smiling Lydia to her feet. Water had splashed the white shirt Lydia was wearing, and it was wet. He was certain that she had no idea he could vividly see her blue bra and the creamy swells of her breasts. His cock was rapidly stirring to attention at the erotic sight.

"Jake . . . Jake!" He blinked as Lydia's voice finally penetrated the sexual fog he'd fallen into. Shit, she still hadn't noticed her shirt, but all of the men in the area had. *Hell, no.* They could get their thrills somewhere else. "Are you coming?" she asked as she turned to follow Casey into the store. *Oh yeah, sweetheart, I'd love to be coming—inside you,* he thought before shaking his head.

"Lydia . . . how about we wait here while you go to the restroom and—freshen up?"

She wrinkled her nose but didn't budge. At this point, one of the nearby men had edged closer and was ogling her tits. Jacob was about two seconds from punching him in the nose, which wouldn't be a great idea with his daughter close by. He glared at the bastard before stepping closer and putting his hand on Lydia's arm. He leaned down until his lips were at her ear and said, "Look at your top, baby. If you don't want me kicking the guy's ass to your left, then please go try to dry it out."

She appeared puzzled for a moment before she warily inspected her clothing. He heard a loud gasp at the same time as her arms quickly came up to cover her breasts. "I . . . I'm going to—be right back," she said shrilly as she hurried away. The nearby man gave him a sheepish look, but thankfully turned in the opposite direction and took off.

"Where Lydie going?" Casey asked, looking forlorn.

He mussed her hair then tweaked her button nose. "She had to go to the restroom, but she'll be right back. How about we go on inside the shop and let you start looking." He knew from painful experience that taking Casey shopping could be a long and drawn-out affair where she would change her mind no less than ten times until she settled on something. He figured he was doing Lydia a favor by letting her get started.

While his daughter darted from one thing to another, he kept watching for Lydia. When he saw her walk into the shop, he raised a hand and drew her attention over to them. His eyes went straight to her chest when she walked up and he could see by the blush on her cheeks that she'd noticed. The area that had been so transparent a short time ago now appeared to be completely dry. "I had to turn it around backward," she confessed as she reached his side. "I tried to use the hand dryer, but it wasn't working very well."

"Er—you look great. No one will know the difference," he assured her then realized he was still gawking at her breasts. "Sorry 'bout that," he murmured, feeling strangely bashful in his admiration for her.

"Ah, no problem." She giggled before Casey ran up and threw herself into Lydia's arms.

"Lydie! You back!" Puckering her small mouth, she said, "Should I get the turtle or the stingray?" Before Lydia could answer, Casey danced around excitedly. "Me knows! I'll get the pink ray and you gets the blue one!" Then she turned those eyes on him, and he was well aware he'd agree to whatever she wanted. *A rainbow pony? Done!* "Daddy, can you buy Lydie a stuffed animal too? I don't know if her got any money or not. But if we buy it for her, then she be our friend forever, right?"

Damn you, Chris, he inwardly raged as he stared at his daughter. She was far too young to believe that she needed to buy friends. No doubt, she had overheard some of her mother's conversations with her cronies. The fact that his impressionable six-year-old attached a dollar figure to loyalty made him queasy. He could tell from the look on Lydia's face that she felt the same way. Before he could gather his wits to talk to her, Lydia had already dropped to her knees to bring her face-to-face with Casey. "Thank you so much, sweetheart, for offering to *loan* me the money for my stuffed animal. That is so very generous and thoughtful of you. I am truly honored to be your friend because of how very special you are. A true friend doesn't need gifts; they only need you. And even when you don't see me every day, I'll still be thinking about how very special you are and wishing you all the best."

Casey stood silently as if digesting Lydia's heartfelt words before she latched on to the last sentence. "You see me at Daddy's, Lydie. I'll ask my mommy if I can come play with you and your ramps."

At that point, Lydia was blinking away tears, and Jake wasn't far behind. A child's simple words were sometimes the hardest to bear, and both he and Lydia were floundering. He straightened his spine and took control, even though it was tough. "All right, girls," he said with false enthusiasm. "Let's finish up in here and go have some lunch. I don't know about you two, but I could eat a whole whale myself!"

Lydia blinked rapidly at the sudden change of conversation, while Casey, with a child's short attention span, rolled with it and ran to grab her pink stingray while handing the blue one to her new friend. Lydia attempted to object, but Jake insisted on paying for both. She'd been amazing with his daughter today, and they both deserved a souvenir to remember their fun. As they stepped back outside into the bright sunlight, Casey took first his hand and then Lydia's as she skipped happily between them. "You know you can't get whale for lunch, silly." She giggled as they swung her off her little feet. "Wheee, again!" she demanded over and over until their arms tired.

This is what it feels like to have a family. The thought struck him suddenly and without forewarning.

He had a great relationship with his parents and his brother, but even though he was a father, he'd never experienced a family moment like this since he became an adult. He'd twirled Casey and she'd ridden on his shoulders countless times, but never with a happy Chris alongside them. This type of behavior was known to irritate her beyond reason. Even at Casey's young age, Chris felt as if she should act like an adult. Jake, on the other hand, wanted his daughter to enjoy being a child. Those carefree years would be gone before any of them knew it, and they could never get them back again.

One of Casey's favorite places was Johnny Rockets. She loved the burgers and milkshakes there, so Jacob ran it past Lydia first to see if the location worked for her and then they walked in that direction. The hostess gave them a big booth, and Casey insisted they all be on the same side so she didn't have to choose who to sit with. As his daughter used the coloring page and crayons to create another masterpiece for his refrigerator, Lydia looked over her head at him and said sweetly, "She's precious, Jake. After one afternoon, I'm totally in love with her."

A sense of pride filled him as he smoothed his daughter's wavy hair. "Regardless of everything with her mother, she's the very air that I breathe," he replied quietly.

Nodding her head in agreement, Lydia said, "I understand why you were willing to do anything to keep from losing her." They both kept an eye on Casey, making sure she wasn't paying attention to their conversation. She appeared to be engrossed in her artwork and have tuned out the rest of the world.

"You were amazing with her today," Jacob said truthfully. "She's always been a little wary around strangers, which I normally encourage for safety reasons, but she connected with you almost immediately."

Lydia appeared touched by his words. "Thanks. I'm an only child, so I've never really been around children much. Brett did have a nephew that we saw at all of the holidays, but that's pretty much the extent of my experience with children. I've always loved them, though, and today was a real treat for me. Seeing a place you've been dozens of times before through the eyes of a child is unbelievable."

They continued to talk throughout the meal whenever they could get in a word around Casey's chatter. By the time they left the restaurant and walked back to the truck, it was nearly time to drop his daughter at home. Casey begged Lydia to sit in the back with her on the drive, and Jacob noticed them cuddled up together through the rearview mirror. If he'd been looking for the perfect stepmother for Casey, he'd found her. They were two peas in a pod. But sadly, all good things had to end, and that time had officially come as he pulled into Chris's driveway and parked behind her BMW.

The house was a modern-style craftsman that Chris complained about constantly. It was in a great neighborhood and a premiere school district, so Jacob ignored her. It also had an amazing fenced backyard, where he knew that his daughter would be safe. Chris would rather live in a trendy condominium, but he'd put his foot down. If he was picking up the tab, then his daughter was going to have the type of house he'd grown up in. As he opened his door and came around to Casey's, he stood awkwardly for a moment. "Lydia—"

"Jake, you don't have to say it. I'm going to move to the front seat and wait for you in the truck. It wouldn't be right for me to barge in there until you've talked to her about me."

Feeling the tension leave his body, Jacob gave her an appreciative wink. "Thanks for understanding, sweetheart. You've been so great today. I don't want to subject you to any more ugliness."

He took his dozing daughter into his arms and heard Lydia close the door behind them as he moved carefully down the walkway with his precious cargo. It appeared to be his lucky night because Chris was on the phone when she answered the door and made no move to end the conversation as she took Casey's hand when he set her on her feet. He gave her a hug and kiss then walked out. He was always sad when he left Casey behind, but somehow, knowing Lydia was waiting for him made it more bearable. She'd been with him for one full day, and already, he was eager to be with her. He hadn't been able to stop thinking of her as his wife today and the need to make that into something other than a title was fast becoming an urge he was having trouble denying.

Chapter Five

Lydia had become good friends with Mia Gentry through their mutual friend and colleague, Crystal. So when Mia had called her at the office and invited her to lunch, Lydia had gratefully accepted. With Crystal away on her honeymoon, Lydia was in desperate need of some girl time. Plus, she was dying to talk to someone about her situation with Jake. The hours they had spent together yesterday, first at the aquarium, and then at dinner, had been one of the best days she'd had in a long time. Being with Jake and Casey had been so easy and natural. When they'd gotten back to his home after dropping Casey off, he'd poured her a glass of wine and he'd had a beer while they talked about their jobs and families.

Of course, it only made sense that she know his background if she was to convince Chris that they had a real marriage. He had assured her that Chris herself didn't know much more about him than a stranger off the street would know. Jake's parents came to see Casey often, but Chris had never visited with them nor had she expressed any interest in doing so. He said that she simply used them as another backup babysitter in the event he was out of town and her parents were unavailable.

Lydia could hardly believe it when Jake had mentioned that it was almost midnight. They'd been sitting and chatting for hours by that point. They'd walked down the hallway together and again he'd had what appeared to be a bashful moment when he stood uncertainly at her door before leaning forward to drop a kiss onto her cheek. "Thanks for today—for everything." She'd stood there fighting the urge to follow him as he headed in the direction of his own room. Sexy Jake's powerful presence was a heady thing to be around, and sweet Jake was melting her inhibitions and her underwear at an alarmingly fast pace. If she wasn't careful, she'd be sneaking into his bed before their first week of marriage was over.

"You look like a woman who's got it bad, sugar," remarked an amused voice. Lydia's eyes flew to the open doorway, where Mia now reclined against the frame. "Don't bother to tell me you're over there pondering a work problem because I won't believe it."

"You had it right the first time," Lydia admitted wryly. Why deny it since she planned on asking her friend for advice during lunch anyway? She got to her feet and pulled her purse from the side drawer of her desk. "Want to walk around the corner to the sandwich shop?" she asked as she moved toward Mia.

"Sounds good to me. I could totally murder a turkey sandwich right now," Mia joked as they rode the elevator down to the lobby. Mia chatted about the latest security system installation she was working on for Danvers while they ordered their food and found a quiet table in the corner.

Despite her earlier statement about being hungry, Mia pushed her sandwich aside after a few bites and asked, "What's going on with Jake? I called you a couple of times over the weekend to check in but kept getting your voice mail."

Lydia dropped her face in her hands and mumbled, "The quick answer is that I'm hopelessly infatuated with him."

"Mmmhmm." Mia smacked her lips. "He's totally fuckable. I'd be more concerned if you didn't feel the way you do."

"I was attracted to him from the start, but now I feel as if I'm just a step away from attacking him," Lydia admitted.

Shrugging her shoulders, Mia asked, "So what's the problem? You're both adults. Make a nookie date and get to it. Hell, you can even have dinner first if you want to keep things civilized."

"I'm living with him," Lydia blurted out. "I agreed to help him with some issues he's having with his daughter's mother."

The bite of food Mia had taken appeared to lodge in her throat as she made a choking sound. Lydia leaned over to thump her on the back until she waved her away. "Jake has a kid? And baby mama drama? Holeee shit! Why am I just now hearing about this? Did you know?" she asked incredulously.

Shaking her head, Lydia said, "Nope, sure didn't. When I left with him after Crystal's wedding, we went to his house to have a chance to talk and he told me everything. He offered to give me an annulment; actually, he wanted to arrange it. Then—"

"Wait." Mia held her hand up. "I thought you guys did the dirty in Vegas. Was he going to lie to avoid going through a divorce?"

Trying to keep any trace of disappointment from her voice, Lydia said, "No, apparently we never had, er . . . intercourse. Which makes sense considering I can remember us fooling around, but it's been driving me crazy that I couldn't recall the main event. He said even intoxicated, he wouldn't let that happen without me being completely sober."

"But it was okay to marry you while you were tipsy?" Mia said dryly.

Lydia felt strangely defensive of her husband, the man she barely knew. "It might not have been the best idea, but we were both in a dismal place that night. I was missing Brett, and what might have been if he hadn't gotten sick. Jake and his ex are pretty close to battling for custody of their daughter. She's saying she'll drop her part if he'll either marry her or pay her more support. And he's determined to get joint custody. He's afraid that his daughter is going to get dragged through a custody case and he doesn't want that to happen to her. He thought if he were married, Chris might back off her demands and the court would look favorably on him if he presented a more settled image, and I just wanted to know what it would feel like to say, 'I do.'" Rubbing at the slight ache in her temples, Lydia admitted, "As insane as it may sound, I was upset when I found out that we hadn't had sex that night and our marriage could be ended so easily. I mean, it's not like I'm in love with him, but he makes me feel desired again. I've been like a robot since Brett died." Pausing, she looked around to make sure no one was listening before continuing, "I haven't . . . you know, wanted anyone sexually in years. But from the moment I met Jake, it's as if my body is some kind of computer that's abruptly come back online."

Mia propped her face in her hand and studied her. Finally, she asked, "So you're going to pretend to be his wife to make him look like a better father? What if he doesn't deserve it? He could be a horrible parent."

"He's an amazing dad," Lydia piped up enthusiastically. "His daughter spent the day with us yesterday. We went to Ripley's Aquarium and then to dinner. She is simply precious, and he hangs on her every word. Their bond was readily apparently whereas the one she has with her mother showed more signs of resignation than affection."

"Whoa," Mia croaked. "You've already met the ex as well? Yikes! How did that go? What's she like?"

Lydia laughed at the rush of questions from her friend. Mia was nothing if not curious. "Well, she's— different," she said, trying to be diplomatic. "She wasn't happy about me being at Jake's house that morning and didn't mind letting it be known. She basically called me a tramp and stomped off in a huff with

Casey. But a few minutes later she was back needing Jake to babysit because she had plans."

Wrinkling her nose, Mia deadpanned, "She sounds awesome. If she was calling you those kind of names so quickly, then she must still have some feelings for our Jake."

Lydia took a drink of her tea before placing it down. "Oh, yeah, she does, but I'm not sure they have anything to do with loving him. According to him, she'd been putting on the pressure in the last year for him to marry her. Then when she never got anywhere with it, she thought attempting to take his daughter away would finally get him where she wanted him."

Mia finished the bite of food that she'd just taken before asking, "If he was willing to marry a stranger, then why not the mother of his child?"

"That's the same thing I asked him," Lydia admitted. "It didn't make sense to me. But he explained how toxic the environment was for Casey when he and Chris were together for any extended amount of time. And just from being in the same room with them for a few minutes, I can see that he's right. Apparently, she was a one-night stand and they never had any type of relationship outside of that before she got pregnant. He believes she's only interested in marrying him for the financial security. Outside of Casey, I don't think they can stand each other."

"Wow, that's sad," Mia sympathized. "It's hard enough on kids when their parents divorce, but when there's not a good relationship to begin with, that must be horrible for everyone involved. Has he told her about his new wife yet?" She looked Lydia up and down before adding, "I assume he hasn't since I don't see any scratches or loss of hair."

Grimacing, Lydia said, "Nope, he didn't want to tell her in front of Casey since she's likely to freak out. He's supposed to talk to her sometime this week, I believe."

Mia leaned back in her chair and wiggled her eyebrows. "Now that we've got all the heavy stuff out of the way, let's circle back to your desire to jump his bones."

"Um . . . what about it?" Lydia asked haltingly. "We don't really know each other. And he probably doesn't think of me in that way. I'm helping him out of a situation and that's it. He hasn't made any moves toward me since we've gotten home."

"Blah, blah, blah." Mia opened and closed her fingers to simulate someone's mouth moving. "Everything doesn't have to be complicated. Sometimes sex can just be about feeling good." Laughing, she added, "Of course, in this instance, Jake married you before he slept with you, so you've already put the proverbial cart before the horse."

Feeling embarrassed, Lydia admitted, "I've only ever been with one man, and we dated for quite a while before we slept together. I loved Brett so much. But . . . I feel something completely different when I'm with Jake." Guiltily, she added, "I was never this sexually aware around Brett. But when Jake is near me, it's almost as if I don't recognize my own body or the intense that he brings out in me. I want him with a force that I've never even experienced—how can he have this kind of effect on me?"

Mia put a hand over hers as she said earnestly, "There is nothing to be ashamed of. The average person loves more than one person in their lifetime and your reactions to two different men will always be different because they aren't the same person. I know it's hard, but you're single, Lydia. There's nothing wrong with you desiring another man." Quirking a brow, she added, "I was going to say every relationship doesn't have to end in marriage, but that's a moot point now."

Lydia giggled, grateful for the comic relief before Mia continued. "Remember when we were talking to Crystal about how lustful she felt toward Mark and how she just needed to go for it?"

"I think it's safe to say she took our advice and then some," Lydia agreed.

Snapping her fingers, Mia said, "Exactly! And now you need to do the same. If you want Jake, then you go after him. And trust me, honey, I saw the way he looked at you at Crystal's wedding. There is no way he's opposed to heating up the sheets with you. If I had to hazard a guess, I'd say he wants you as much or more than you want him."

"Really?" Lydia blinked, hardly able to believe Mia could have the right read on the situation. Was Jake feeling the same pull of physical attraction?

"Oh, yeah." Mia nodded. "Now, I want you to go forth and seduce that man. And trust me, there won't be any challenge there. He might feel like he can't approach you because you're doing him a favor by helping with his custody situation. But if you crook your finger and let him know that you're ready and willing, he'll come running."

"I don't know," Lydia murmured uncertainly. "What if I do and he turns me down? I'd feel like a fool, and I'd have to face him every day after that."

Shaking her head empathically, Mia said, "I'm telling you, he won't. Outside of the fact that you're a beautiful woman, you're also flipping hot."

"You're just saying that because you're my friend." Lydia felt sure that the other woman couldn't have said it with any kind of sincerity.

Mia shrugged her shoulders as if she were talking about the weather. "Honey, look at yourself in the mirror. You have the kind of hourglass figure that every man fantasizes about. Big boobs, small waist, and a squeezable booty. Old Jake has probably damned near worn his hand out in the last twenty-four hours with you under the same roof!"

Lydia wanted to crawl under the table when she saw a group of men at a nearby table begin to snicker while darting glances their way. She had no doubt they'd heard some of the more embarrassing parts of their conversation. "Oh God, they're listening to us," she whispered to Mia as she nodded her head toward the other table.

Uncaring of the attention, Mia turned her head and faced the eavesdroppers without batting an eye. "Hey, dudes," she called out. Instantly, they fixated on her as if waiting anxiously for her next words. Of course, the fact that Mia was gorgeous probably didn't hurt any. "Since you guys are obviously catching some of our discussion, how about giving us your honest opinion."

"Oh shit," Lydia moaned in horror, terrified of what was going to come out of her friend's mouth. There was no way it would be good.

One of the men, who'd apparently appointed himself the spokesperson for the group, leaned forward and smiled. "We're always happy to assist pretty ladies. What can we help you with?"

Mia turned to Lydia and uttered under her breath, "Just remember, this is for your own good." Clearing her throat, Mia moved her chair closer to the other table and lowered her voice. "Do you see my friend over there?" When they nodded, she asked, "How many of you would go out with her if given the chance?" As Lydia was in the process of wilting into her chair, she saw something mind-boggling. The hand of every guy at the table flew up as if shot from a cannon.

One even replied enthusiastically, "Any day, anywhere, sweetheart."

Mia clapped her hands. "I have just one more question. What word would you use to describe her? And keep it fairly clean, boys."

A chorus of voices rang out as Lydia heard, "Hot," "sexy," "stunning," and "beautiful." Her mind was officially blown, and she barely registered that Mia had resumed her seat and was looking at her expectedly.

Holding up a hand, the other woman said, "I know you may have the urge to punch me, but I wanted you to see yourself the way others see you. Those men look successful and they're certainly handsome. I doubt they have a problem picking up women. But they were damn near falling out of their seats at a chance to sing your praises. Trust me, they might have tried to come up with something passably nice to say if they hadn't found you attractive, but that didn't happen. They were effusive in their praise, and they were more than interested in asking you out."

When Lydia remained skeptical, Mia opened her hand and dropped a stack of cards on the table. Puzzled, Lydia asked, "What are those?"

Mia gave her a satisfied smirk. "The business card of every dude at the table. Some even wrote down all their numbers so you could reach them anywhere."

Lydia's jaw dropped in shock. She glanced at the nearby table, only to have one good-looking man with beautiful eyes wink at her. She knew she was blushing like an idiot, but strangely, it felt good to be admired. Had she been so tuned out that she hadn't noticed male attention all of this time? She'd never looked at another man when she was with Brett, and after he died, she certainly had no interest in the opposite sex. She hadn't realized that somehow she'd translated that lack of interest on her part into some sort of insecurity. She wasn't interested in dating. Therefore, she wasn't datable. Wow, when had it gotten to that point?

This crazy experiment of Mia's had shown her exactly how twisted her self-perception had become. She wasn't ready to admit that she was a raving beauty because she certainly didn't feel that way. But like every woman out there, didn't she have something that worked for her? A feature that men found attractive. Wasn't it possible that Jake would desire her? And as Mia had pointed out, did she have anything to lose by letting him know that she certainly was drawn to him. "You're getting it now, aren't you?" Mia practically purred in satisfaction. "You have that look that says 'I am woman, hear me roar.'"

"I don't know about that," Lydia giggled, "but I may possibly concede that I have more to offer than I originally thought." Schooling her expression into a frown, she added, "Although I'm not condoning your methods, I am strangely happy with the results."

Mia held up a hand, patiently waiting for Lydia to give her a high five. With her mouth twitching, Lydia finally gave in when her friend rolled her lips out in an elaborate pout. "Yeah!" Mia crowed. Tossing a look over her shoulders where the men still lingered, she said in an undertone, "Now, let's get out of here before they follow us back to the office. I'm almost certain I've heard the word 'threesome' a few times, and I'd hate to knee one of them in the balls since they were so helpful."

Lydia got to her feet and hurried after Mia's departing form. She couldn't help smiling a little bigger when the men all threw their hands up and waved eagerly as she passed their table. Score one for Mia. Lydia had left the office for lunch feeling hopelessly attracted to Jacob, but resigned to the fact that nothing would ever happen there. Now, even with the possibility that he might still turn her down, but she was determined to give it her best shot. And she owed her newfound confidence to an amazingly outspoken friend and a handful of strangers who'd been kind enough to give her the confidence that she'd hadn't even realized she'd been missing.

It's time to seduce my hubby tonight. Game on, Mr. Hay—game on.

Jake knew it was cowardly, but instead of driving to Chris's house to talk, he'd asked her to meet him at the country club for lunch. Personally, he'd hated most of the pompous crowd that gravitated toward the place, but he also knew that Chris was less likely to cause a scene among the people whose admiration she so coveted. *Know thy enemy.* Not a terribly nice thought about the mother of his child, but experience had taught him a tough lesson there. Chris was a born drama queen on her best days, and this wasn't likely to be one of those.

He pulled into the parking lot and glanced around until he located her car. He took an available spot a few spaces down and slid out of his truck. She'd obviously decided to head on inside since her vehicle was empty. He was pathetically grateful for the small reprieve before facing her. To say she was going to be livid would be an understatement. Judging by her reaction to meeting Lydia at his house on Sunday, she would probably go postal over the wedding news.

A big part of him still wondered if he should be going forward with this deception—because that's what it was. Lydia, out of the goodness of her heart, had agreed to help him, and even though he'd put up some token protests, he'd still jumped at the opportunity. He'd lain awake most of last night thinking about her. He hadn't been able to get the last time he'd touched her in Vegas out of his head. He wondered what her reaction would be if she knew he'd jacked off to the memory of going down on her for the first time. The sounds of her moans still filled his head. What he wouldn't give to taste her again.

"You're late," said an annoyed voice. To his chagrin, he jumped as Chris glared down at her watch.

"Sorry," he offered, not really meaning it. He'd probably wasted what amounted to a year of his life by now waiting for her when she was late dropping off Casey, so he didn't feel any remorse for keeping her waiting. The hostess led them to a relatively quiet table in the corner and Jacob automatically held out Chris's chair for her. They both remained quiet until they'd ordered. He had a burger and she had some kind of salad with the dressing on the side. It reminded him of dinner with Lydia and Casey at Johnny Rockets. He'd been thrilled to see a woman actually eating a hearty meal. He loved her soft curves and womanly figure. Chris was even thinner than she'd been the first time they met, and she'd been too skinny then. Most men would certainly consider her attractive, and apparently, he'd been one of them since he slept with her. But if you looked below the surface, it was all superficial. She was the type that never left the house without being perfectly dressed with flawless makeup. There was no way she'd have been lying on her stomach at an aquarium petting stingrays with her daughter.

He caught her giving him a calculating look before she carefully schooled her expression. "So what's the occasion?" she asked casually. "We don't normally meet alone for a meal."

It was then he saw it. She thought she had him. She figured this whole lunch was about him throwing in the towel and caving to her demands. *You're in for such a disappointment, sweetheart.* He took a drink of his water and wished belatedly that he'd ordered a beer. *Something to be said for liquid courage.* Clearing his throat, he began, "I wanted to talk to you today while Casey was in school. She's seen you and me argue far too much, and I refuse to keep doing it." He could see by the frown on her face that the importance of his words was sinking in. He wouldn't have said what he had if he'd been planning to marry her.

"Get to the point," she bit out stiffly, looking as if she wouldn't mind an alcoholic beverage herself.

Here goes. Brace for impact. "The woman you met at my home yesterday is actually my wife. Lydia and I were married—"

"What!" she hissed, all color draining from her face. *"Your wife?* How is that even possible?"

He winced as she ground her teeth together. She appeared to be approaching apocalyptic levels a lot faster than he'd imagined. People at nearby tables were already darting curious glances their way. Possibly this public meeting hadn't been a good idea after all. "Lydia is my wife," he inserted calmly. "And I'd appreciate it if you didn't refer to her as a tramp again because I can assure you that she isn't. I also must insist that you not say things like that around my daughter. You realize that she's likely repeating that garbage at school, right?"

"*Your wife!*" she screeched yet again, bringing the conversations around them to a halt.

"Chris, lower your voice," he instructed. "You're making a spectacle of yourself."

"I could give a fuck!" she snapped. "How dare you bring me here and unload something like this on me!" She leaned so far into the table her chest was sitting in her salad plate. He certainly didn't have the nerve to point that out, though. She'd probably throw the damn thing if he brought it to her attention. "You know what, Jake, I don't believe you," she taunted. "I think you're lying your ass off to get me off your back. What did you think—I'd just say, 'Well, hey, congratulations to you both. I wish you all the best'?"

"A guy could hope," he joked, then wiped the smile quickly off his face when her left eye began twitching. Wow, he'd always known she was tightly strung, but he was ready to call for an exorcist. He was afraid she'd climb on the table at any moment and attempt to stab him with her salad fork. And the profanity, that was another shocker. Obviously, she was fond of the word "tramp," but the string of curse words she was muttering under her breath were new. As were the insults she was now heaping upon his mother. *Holy hell.* As he looked around to see the entire place riveted on them, he closed his eyes and took a breath. He had to get her out of here before they called the cops.

"Christine!" he said harshly. Thankfully, the tone

of his voice instantly cut through her tirade, and she paused long enough for him to continue. "If you'll stop for one moment, you'll notice that anyone and everyone that you've ever wanted to impress are staring at you as if you've lost your mind. Now, I'm leaving before we are hauled out of here in handcuffs. I'd suggest that you do the same." He saw the moment it hit her. Her cheeks turned a vivid shade of red, and she dropped her eyes to the linen tablecloth.

"You bastard," she whispered. "This is all your fault. I've put six years into you and you go and marry some piece of trash off the street? We could have been a family. But nooo, you had to ruin everything." Getting to her feet, she glared down at him as she attempted to brush the stain from the mixed greens from her silk top. "You'll pay for this," she threatened before turning to stalk off.

Their waiter came hurrying over as if she'd been waiting for a break in the action. She efficiently picked up the mess that Chris had made without comment. Then she turned to him and raised a brow. "Can I get you anything else, sir?"

With a snort, he said, "How about a Jack and Coke?"

She broke her polite expression long enough to smile at him before saying, "That sounds like an excellent idea, sir."

A few short moments later, he sat sipping his drink and waiting for the calm it would hopefully bring. If he were an optimistic man, he'd say it was over and he'd gotten the hard part out of the way. But with Chris, he was dearly afraid that he hadn't really seen anything yet. Tonight, he needed to warn Lydia to beware not only of things that go bump in the night, but also of ex-girlfriends who lose their shit during the daylight hours. *Never sleep with anyone crazier than you are.* Those were words he had definitely come to regret not living by.

Chapter Six

Lydia used the garage remote that Jake had given her that morning along with the house key and alarm code. Within moments, she was parked and walking into her temporary home. She hadn't been sure what Jake had in mind for their dinner plans, so she'd stopped on the way home and picked up the ingredients for spaghetti—didn't everyone love pasta? Geez, she hoped he wasn't on some low-carb eating plan. He certainly had a body that would attest to a careful diet and exercise. Her own curvy figure gave testament to the fact she enjoyed her food and didn't deprive herself of indulgences as often as she probably should.

She had changed into a pair of soft yoga pants and a tank top before returning to the kitchen to boil the noodles and make the sauce—which was out of a jar tonight. She did add some extra spices to liven it up a bit.

Jake walked in the door just as she was plating her food. She noted he looked a bit tired, but otherwise just as delectable as he had that morning. He gave her a smile before removing his suit jacket and draping it over a bar stool. "How was your day?" he asked as he sniffed the air appreciatively. "Wow, that smells amazing. Better than my usual fare."

"My day was good," she replied as she filled another plate for him. She figured since it was just the two of them, they could eat at the bar. "I hope you like spaghetti. It's nothing fancy, but it sounded good."

"Sweetheart, it's wonderful." He touched her shoulder as he walked by. "I'll grab a bottle of wine from the rack. Would you like a glass?"

Nodding, she said, "Yes, please." They worked around each other as if they'd been doing it for years, and soon, they'd settled side by side twirling pasta onto their forks. When Jake moaned his approval after his first bite, Lydia felt her body spark to life. What she wouldn't give to hear him make that sound while they were between the sheets together. Heck, she had heard it before; she'd just been too drunk to appreciate how sexy it sounded.

Between mouthfuls, he joked, "I'd marry you if we weren't already hitched. It's nice to come home to a meal that I didn't have to cook or place an order for. Thank you for doing this," he added sincerely.

"So how was your day?" she asked as she sipped her wine.

"It sucked," he deadpanned.

She blinked rapidly at him, unsure if she'd heard correctly. "Really?" she finally asked when he didn't elaborate. "Did something happen or was it just one of those days?"

He took a few more bites of pasta and wiped his mouth with his napkin before turning his chair toward hers. "I had lunch with Chris today and told her the happy news. Let me just say we're probably not getting a congratulations card in the mail anytime soon. She'd be more likely to egg our house or paper our trees."

Lydia choked back the thrill she got at him using the word "our" to focus on what he'd said. "Wow, I'm sorry," she said simply. "I mean, you didn't think she'd be happy about it, so why are you surprised?"

Rubbing his chin, he chuckled dryly. "She went about fifty levels above how I thought she would react, especially in a public place. The country club is probably going to cancel my membership after the show we put on for them. Chris was tossing out profanities faster than a speeding bullet. She involved everyone from the Holy Father to my mother."

"Why in the world would you go somewhere like that to talk to her?" Lydia asked in confusion. That was like sitting on a church pew with your cell phone volume turned to high. Was he that naïve to think she wouldn't show her ugly side in public? *Men—they always underestimate a woman scorned.*

"I thought she was less likely to freak out if she was around other social climbers. She's usually paranoid about her image and trying to be one of the society crowd. I had no idea she'd start frothing at the mouth at the word 'married.' Of course, I expected her to be upset, but damn, it was almost like some kind of breakdown. She might not be pleasant most of the time, but this was in a whole new zip code from her usual neighborhood of irritated behavior." Wincing, he added, "At one point, she told me she'd like to 'shove my balls up my ass and choke me with them in reverse,' or something along those lines."

Lydia couldn't help it when she burst out laughing. She could picture Jake sitting there surrounded by people enjoying their lunches while Chris spewed profane and creative insults his way. She would bet he wouldn't make the mistake of having a public meeting about a touchy subject with her again. Chris must have completely lost it when she'd discovered that she wasn't going to get her way with him, no matter how much she threatened him with his daughter. Looking at Jake sitting just inches away, so damn handsome it should be a sin, she could almost sympathize with the other woman. His thick, dark hair was standing on end in several places as if he'd run his hands through it more than once during the day. His eyes—which reminded her of a vivid blue sky on a summer's day— were smiling at her, not in the least upset that she'd just been laughing at his painful experience with Chris. And those lips. God, they drove her crazy. They seemed unusually full for a man and so utterly kissable. Heck, she'd thought multiple times about sucking the bottom one into her mouth and—

"I swear, baby, you need to stop whatever you're thinking because you're killing me," Jake said roughly.

Busted. From Jake's pained expression, she figured what she'd been feeling had been written all over her face. Talk about awkward. Did she laugh it off and pretend it had nothing to do with him, even though she might have moaned his name at some point without knowing it? No, surely, she hadn't been that out of it. A denial was on the tip of her tongue when she remembered her conversation with Mia. Even though she hadn't planned it, this gave her an opening if she wanted to pursue more of a physical relationship with Jake. And if his reaction was any indication, he wasn't averse to it. *You can do this. The worst that can happen is he says no.* Pulling up the proverbial big girl panties, she met his gaze head-on and said, "What if I don't want to stop?"

He was shocked; that much was readily apparent by his sharp intake of breath. But there was more. He wanted her. His eyes were like twin sapphires of fire. And the hand that had been lying relaxed on the bar was now clenched tightly. "Make sure you mean it, Lydia. Don't start something you won't see through."

Taking a huge leap of faith, she got to her feet and eased between his spread legs until they were almost chest to chest. "I want you, Jake," she whispered.

Please let him take over now before my bravado deserts me.

With a muttered oath, his arms encircled her and his hands came to rest on the cheeks of her ass. Pulling her even closer, he lowered his head and took her lips. It soon became apparent that he wasn't a man to play around. His tongue didn't ask permission—it staked a claim as it entered her mouth. She'd never been this turned on from a kiss, but as he licked, nipped, and sucked, her clit fluttered madly to life. As caught up in the moment as she was, a part of her mind was still waiting for him to move the show into the bedroom. But Jake, it seemed, had other plans. With agility that would put a circus performer to shame, he moved his hands to her waist and hoisted her onto the granite countertop—all without releasing her lips. In fact, he kept possession of those until he put a hand behind her head and began easing her backward, laying her across the cool surface. He took a step back and just stared down at her. "You are so fucking beautiful," he said huskily as he trailed a finger between her breasts and down her stomach. He eased the fabric of her blouse from her slacks and began opening the buttons with a skill that was impressive. *This isn't his first rodeo; he knows his way around a woman's clothing.*

As he parted the fabric and revealed her lacy pink bra, she lay in breathless anticipation of his next move. He raised his hands and cupped her breasts, teasing the hardening nipples through the thin material. "Oh God," she hissed as desire flooded her core. *I'm going to come before he even touches me down there*, she thought but couldn't bring herself to care. It had been too long since she'd felt a man's hands on her body, and she hadn't realized how much it would affect her. The first time they'd been together, she'd been intoxicated. Tonight, she was high on nothing but him and the way he made her feel. When he abruptly tugged the cups of her bra down and released her swollen peaks, she moaned her approval. Then he sucked one into his mouth, biting it hard enough to leave a stinging sensation. "Jake! Sooo good," she cried as her orgasm ripped through her body.

Instead of continuing to lavish attention upon her hardened peaks, he surprised her by shifting down her body and pulling her slacks and underwear off in one impressive move. She'd removed her shoes earlier, so nothing stopped them from pooling to the floor. Then he was circling her slick cleft before burying one thick digit inside her. "Ride my hand, baby, take what you need," he ordered roughly—and she did. Out of her mind with desire, she gripped the edge of the counter and moved her body downward, while he thrust upward and into her wet heat. "That's it, sweet-heart," he rasped out. She was right there, just seconds away from coming again, until he laid an arm across her hips and stilled her movements. "I own this one, sweetheart, let me finish you." He took her feet and swung them over his shoulders before lowering his mouth to devour her dripping sex. He continued to move his finger in and out of her while he took her throbbing clit into his mouth and sucked.

"Oh, my God, Jake!" she screamed as she fisted his hair and held on for dear life. Even when she tried to pull away, he refused to let her. He kept working her until nothing was left of her orgasm but an occasional shudder. "That was . . . wow," she whispered in awe. She heard Jake's muffled laughter and realized she still held him captive between her thighs. Releasing her hold on his hair, she grinned sheepishly at him. "Er, sorry about that."

He laughed easily as he dropped a kiss on one of her thighs, which still hung over his shoulders. "You'll never hear me complain about being trapped there, sweetheart. It's about as close to heaven as I can imagine."

She was basking in the beauty of his words when he began peeling his clothing off. She swallowed audibly as he locked his eyes on hers. He pulled his shirt from his pants and tossed it on the floor, followed quickly by his undershirt. *Come to Mama*, she thought heatedly as her mouth watered at the sight of broad shoulders that tapered down into washboard abs. You could easily bounce a quarter off that firm flesh. "Nice," she squeaked inadequately. What did one say in response to something like that? She was sure a poet somewhere would do it justice, but for now, her one-word mumblings would have to do.

The sound of him unbuckling his belt was like a gunshot in the kitchen. Followed closely by the unmistakable swish of his zipper lowering. They were really doing this. He was going to take her right where they'd had a bowl of spaghetti moments earlier. *How smoking hot!* A man was so impatient for her, he couldn't make it to the bedroom. She'd had fantasies about sex like this for years. The craziest place she'd ever done it to date was in the shower and even that had been only a couple of times. Brett believed in making love in the bedroom or occasionally on the sofa. Certainly not in the kitchen. "You have no idea how much I've wanted this," Jake growled. She watched in amazement as he pulled his wallet out and removed a condom from it. Apparently, every man did walk around with a rubber *just in case*.

Lydia found herself trying to subtly strain to see his size as he shoved his pants then boxer briefs down.

When his cock bounced up toward his stomach, her breath came out in a whistle. *Dear mother of all things big and long.* Granted, she'd slept with only one man before, so she had limited experience, but she'd been certain that monster cocks like that didn't really exist. That was why they made vibrators so big, right? Then a girl could have a man with a regular-size dick and enjoy something a little more substantial when she was in the mood for variety. Only now, she knew she'd been wrong—in a big way. She gulped, and then continued with the one-word utterances. "Big." He cocked a brow at her as he fisted his cock. "Huge," she added as if that sounded any better. The man was probably starting to believe he was having sex with an idiot incapable of stringing more than two words together to form a coherent thought.

He gave her a wolfish grin as he actually wiggled his massive penis in her direction before sliding on a condom with the other hand. *Extra-large size, no doubt.* Then he was grabbing her legs in each hand and spreading them wider. And back over his shoulders they went. He seemed to really have a thing for that position. When the fat head of his cock brushed against her slit, she moaned like a porn star on her first audition. She was afraid her starved sex was going to grab his staff and pull him inside before he ever had the chance to thrust. That absurd thought had her on the verge of giggling until he pushed inside her balls deep with no warning. "Fuck!" he hissed as if in pain.

"Ahhh, Jake," she moaned as her body rushed to accommodate his size. If not for the fact that she was still soaking wet from their foreplay, his sudden entry would have been painful. As it was, her sex burned as it stretched around his massive size. But on the other side of that discomfort was a pleasure the likes of which she'd never experienced before. He pulled out then pushed back in deep once again and held himself there. He leaned closer, grinding his pubic bone against her. *My husband is a sex god. I've hit the jackpot or maybe that's jackcock.*

"You okay, sweetheart?" he rasped out as he circled his hips against her. She nodded frantically, unable to spit out even the single-word responses she had been managing. He made a series of shallow thrusts before plunging back in once again. Then she felt his finger rubbing her clit and she detonated. And she kept contracting around him as he gave two more fast pumps before finding his own release with a harsh shout of pleasure.

In her post-coital bliss, Lydia was only vaguely aware of being carried through the house. She was surprised, though, when instead of walking to the bedroom that she'd used the previous night, Jake went to his instead. He shifted her in his arms to pull the comforter back on the bed, before laying her body on the cool sheets. "This feels nice," she murmured as she snuggled into the softness.

She had almost drifted off to sleep when he reappeared at her side, nudging her legs apart. She felt a warm cloth wiping her there, and as much as she wanted to be embarrassed about the intimacy of it, she figured that reaction was silly since his dick had just been inside her not five minutes ago. It didn't get much more personal than that. "Slide over, baby," he instructed as he laid a hand on her hip. She shifted to make room for his large frame in the bed. She was both surprised and blissfully happy when he turned her onto her side and spooned against her back. "What time is it?" she asked drowsily, thinking it couldn't be terribly late.

"It's just after nine." He chuckled. "I haven't turned in for the night this early in years."

"Oh no, we just left all of our dishes sitting in the kitchen," she mumbled. "I need to clean up before we go to sleep."

"Relax, sweetheart," he said, pulling her firmly against him. "I put everything in the dishwasher before I locked up."

Those were the last words she heard before she fell into an exhausted slumber.

Jake lay awake long after Lydia had drifted off to sleep. He certainly hadn't planned on what had happened between them earlier, but by God, it had been so incredibly hot. Her response to his touch had been perfect. He'd been strangely moved when he'd come home from work to find her in his kitchen making dinner. Such a domestic situation should have scared the hell out of him. Instead, he'd found himself grateful to her for being there after his lunch altercation with Chris. Just talking and laughing about it all had felt so damn good. He'd never had any desire for something like that, but for the first time, he wondered what else he'd been missing out on by avoiding relationships.

Then she had given him that look. One that quite plainly said she wanted him. He'd even warned her to stop if she didn't mean it, but she hadn't backed down. He'd been so eager, he'd almost lost control a few times—which never happened to him. He'd had to recite a lot of baseball statistics in his head and thankfully it had worked.

Afterward, without even thinking, he'd brought her to his room instead of hers. Another oddity—he didn't spend the night with women and he damn sure didn't spoon them as he was doing now. But she'd been different from anyone else he'd been with from the beginning in a way that he didn't fully comprehend. And truthfully after the mind-blowing sex and the need to be close to her, he was a little lost.

He didn't have a clue as to what to do next, and as the hours ticked away, he got increasingly nervous about facing what was sure to be some morning-after awkwardness. So, an hour earlier than usual he slid quietly from the bed and took a quick shower before dressing in the closet with the door closed. He hadn't even bothered to shave.

He felt like an asshole as he crept through the still dark bedroom and out the door. But the only thing he felt sure of was that he needed the day to regroup. If there was any chance that he and Lydia might have something between them other than a marriage in name only, then he needed to find a way to stop freaking out at the first sign of intimacy.

When Lydia woke up the next morning, Jake was already gone. She looked around thinking maybe he'd left her a note. But no, the only indication that anything had happened last night was the tenderness between her legs and the fact that she was in his bed.

Then it hit her that possibly he was just in another part of the house, maybe making some coffee. So, not seeing any clothing on the floor, she quickly pulled the sheet from the bed and wrapped it around herself before going to investigate. A few moments and a quick peek into the garage later she had her answer—he'd left without a word to her. *What did you expect? A letter with hearts written by your name? This is Jacob Hay, he doesn't do romance.*

Hitching the bedding up tighter under her arms, she released a disappointed sigh before moving to the coffeepot and turning it on. She walked back to the bedroom and into the bathroom to take a shower while the coffee was brewing. As the hot water cascaded over her, she let her mind drift to the previous evening. Jake had set her body afire in a way that she'd never dreamed was possible. As mind blowing as the sex had been, though, it had been the surprisingly tender gesture of him holding her close in his bed afterward that had really touched her. Maybe that's why waking up alone this morning had shocked her. Obviously, she'd expected a bit more from him today. If nothing else, some kind of acknowledgment of their night together would have been nice.

Was that expecting too much from a man who had openly admitted to never having had a serious relationship? The current situation was something new for them both. They were attracted to each other and had acted on it. Did it have to be more than that at this point? She'd married Jake in a drunken Las Vegas moment. There was nothing traditional about it. So instead of the hurt that she had originally felt at his absence, she did something she wouldn't normally do. She decided to live in the moment for as long as possible. She had to believe that Jake had come into her life for a reason and she could either embrace their time together or make herself miserable by overanalyzing everything that occurred.

God, hadn't she spent enough time being unhappy?

Turning off the shower, Lydia stepped out and squared her shoulders. She'd had kick-ass sex last night. For today, that's all she needed to focus on.

Chapter Seven

Lydia stood on the sidewalk holding a large gift bag while she waited for Crystal to pick her up. They were attending a baby shower for Suzy Merimon. She and her husband, Gray, had adopted an adorable little boy they'd named John Nicholas Merimon. They'd actually been present for his birth and had taken him home from the hospital with them almost two months ago. Lydia had liked the outspoken Suzy from their very first meeting, and she couldn't wait to see her again today. Danvers International wasn't the same with her on maternity leave.

As she stared off into the distance, her thoughts turned to Jake. They had been living together now for almost three weeks and the most surprising thing had happened. They acted just like a normal, married couple. Lydia had taken to making dinner most evenings, and more often than not, Jake was home to join her. Afterward, they would talk about their day, and if Jake didn't have work to do, they would watch a movie. And they continued to make love every evening. She'd considerably broadened her horizon and could now add sex on the bathroom counter, against the wall, and in the laundry room.

Jake, it seemed, was insatiable. She had averaged having sex maybe a few times per week before Brett had gotten sick, and after that, it had been almost non-existent. But since she moved in with Jake, they hadn't missed a single day. Sometimes more than once. He was surprisingly affectionate and considerate out of the bedroom as well.

Even Chris had been low-key regarding her presence in Jake's life, which was unexpected. Casey had visited them several times, but her mother had been sullen on both occasions. Lydia had a bad feeling it was possibly the calm before the storm, but she didn't want to burst Jake's hopeful bubble. As uncertain as things were, the one thing that Lydia was positive about was that she adored Jake's daughter. They'd bonded so easily and quickly that it was as if they'd been in each other's lives for years. She knew that she should try to keep some distance between them, but she just couldn't. She didn't know how she would survive not seeing the little girl again when Jake no longer needed her. The mere thought of not being a part of either of their lives was like a knife to her soul.

When Crystal pulled up to the curb and honked her horn, Lydia almost jumped out of her skin. Wow, she hadn't realized she was that zoned out. She walked around the Mercedes C-Class that Mark had insisted on buying Crystal when they had gotten engaged. He didn't feel that her other car was safe enough. Crystal had disagreed, of course, because she loved her Volkswagen Beetle, but in the end, it hadn't been worth the argument, she'd said. As Lydia slid onto the sleek leather, she thought her friend had made the right decision.

"Hey, buddy," Crystal called out before leaning across the seat to hug her. Even though they had talked on the phone for almost an hour the previous night, they hadn't seen each other since Crystal had returned from her honeymoon a few days earlier and Lydia had missed her terribly. "How are you?" Pulling back, Crystal studied her intently for a moment. "You look amazing. You're glowing in a way I've never seen before."

Lydia laughed. "You're the one who just got back from two weeks with your dream guy. I think if anyone could light up the night, it would be you!"

Crystal smiled dreamily and nodded. "Yeah, I'm beyond happy. I never thought I could feel like this. After being married to someone as reserved and downright cold as Bill, I always thought every relationship was that way." Wiggling her eyebrows, she giggled. "Boy, was I wrong! Marriage to Mark is the polar opposite. He's amazing both in and out of bed." With a sigh of contentment, she added, "I feel like I can be the me I've always wanted to be with him. Does that sound crazy?"

"Not in the least," Lydia assured her wryly. "I feel the same with Jake, and we're just pretending to be married. Is it totally weird that being with him is as natural as breathing to me? I mean we're basically strangers who got married for none of the right reasons, but it feels so right." Before Crystal could answer, Lydia moaned and dropped her head forward. "Don't bother to answer, that sounds insane even to me."

"Hey." Crystal nudged her arm. "Who's to say what's normal? I think that's up to each couple to decide. Are you happy?"

Lifting her head, Lydia couldn't stop the no doubt sappy smile that filled her face. "The last few weeks have been magical for me. I have a husband who comes home at the end of the day and a daughter that keeps me laughing. Jake and I have developed a routine that seems so easy. Which scares the hell out of me," she finished with a sigh.

"Because you don't want it to end," Crystal guessed accurately.

"Bingo." Lydia nodded. "I've taken to this life as if I were made for it. But there's a big clock ticking, and as soon as Chris backs off and Jake doesn't feel threatened anymore, then he'll be ready to get back to however he was living before I came along."

Crystal put one hand on the steering wheel, and it was then that Lydia realized they were still sitting in front of Jake's house. Glancing down at her watch, she cried, "Oh crap! We've been talking for so long that we're already ten minutes late! You know how Suzy is—she might lock us out of her house for this."

Crystal giggled, but promptly put the car in gear and pulled out onto the road. "Yeah, we don't want to be the last ones to arrive. Luckily for us, Ella is usually always running late now with Sofia, so we may be okay. Anyway, back to your last comment. You and Jake have been sleeping together every day basically since you moved in. Don't you think he's forming some attachments to the living arrangement as well? I mean I know that, like Mark, Jake hasn't really been involved in serious relationships. But that can change for the right person. Don't assume that he's not experiencing some of what you are."

"You're saying I shouldn't keep my suitcase sitting at the front door just in case he decides to keep me?" Lydia joked.

Groaning, Crystal said, "That wasn't exactly the way I would have worded it, but you've got the basic message down. If you're happy with what's happening between you two, then keep going with it. Don't start mentioning some kind of expiration date to him. Why plant ideas in his head, where there may well be none? I read an article in *Cosmo* the other day that said never to point out your flaws to a man because, eventually, they might start to believe your version over their own."

"Well, I'm not walking around mentioning the size of my butt to him," Lydia joked.

Snorting, Crystal said, "That's good to know. But I think you see where I'm going with this advice. Absolutely enjoy yourself and don't stress over tomorrow."

"I'm trying," Lydia assured her. "Grabbing the bull by the horns and all those other things they say to do as a fearless, modern female."

"Oh, I think you've grabbed on to something," Crystal sniggered, "but it looks like more of a stallion." They were both still giggling like teenagers when they reached Suzy's home. She lived only a few miles away from Jake's house in Garden City Beach.

As they left the car and made their way up the steps, Claire, the wife of Jason Danvers, the CEO of Danvers International, opened the front door. She was a stunning blonde who always had a ready smile for everyone around the office. Lydia had heard that she'd actually been Jason's assistant at one time. If that didn't have fairy-tale romance written all over it, she didn't know what did. "Hey, guys." Claire smiled brightly. "I'm so glad you could make it." Lowering her voice, she whispered, "Little John just barfed all over Suzy so there's a bit of a commotion. She hasn't quite gotten used to being drenched when you least expect it."

"I'm not sure anyone adjusts to that," said an amused voice as Beth Merimon joined them. "I think it's pretty funny, though. Because every time Henry spits up or poops, she hands him off as if he's on fire." Rubbing her hands together in obvious glee, Beth added, "Those days are over for my sister, though. She gets to experience all the delights that motherhood has to offer!"

As they made their way into the foyer, Ella hustled up with her daughter, Sofia, in her arms. Lydia had always thought that Crystal's sister was gorgeous, and today was no exception. A certain innocence about her made her even more appealing. She could see why Ella's husband—former playboy Declan Stone—was intrigued by someone so opposite from him. Lydia knew that an overbearing mother in a very restricted environment had raised both Ella and Crystal. It had taken a lot of courage, but they had managed to break away and, in doing so, had found their soul mates. "I was wondering where you were, sis," Ella called out as she stepped forward to wrap an arm around Crystal. "I missed you so much."

"It sure doesn't look like she was pining away for any of us on her honeymoon," Emma Davis inserted as she joined their group. Emma was engaged to Declan's brother, Brant, and was soon to be part of the Stone family. "If that satisfied expression on your face is any indication, then you and Mark had a great time. Did you ever actually leave your room?"

"Oh, good Lord, here we go with the sex talk," replied Ava Powers, a sleek blonde. Truthfully, it had taken Lydia months to match all of the women with the men at Danvers that they were either married or engaged to. Ava was married to Mac Powers, who ran East Coast Security, along with Dominic Brady and Gage Hyatt. Dominic was engaged to Gwen, who was also close friends with Crystal and Mia. Funnily enough, Gwen had once dated Mac before he finally landed the woman he'd loved since childhood—Ava. It was enough to make Lydia's head spin just trying to keep the details straight. The fact that they all seemed to be a big, extended happy family was equal parts amazing and downright crazy.

"Oh, come on, Ava, everyone here likes to talk smut except for you. And I see the way you roll into the office some mornings, so I know that you and Mac aren't sitting around knitting in the evening." Emma was Ava's assistant at Danvers, and Lydia thought it was hysterical how they bickered like sisters.

Ava looked down, studying her nails as she said, "Not all of us kiss and tell, Em. You could take a page on discretion from my book. I'm sure my brother would be happy if you stopped telling the world how big his—er, equipment is."

Mia swiveled her hips as she walked up. "I personally like hearing about pecker sizes. If we could convince the men to do a 'Studs of Danvers' calendar, we'd all be rich. I'd even convince Seth to do an honorary appearance."

"Oh, brother," Gwen moaned as she shifted her baby boy on her shoulder. Cameron McKinley Powers was named after Dominic's two business partners and was simply gorgeous. Instead of Gwen's red hair, he had his father's dark coloring. The fact that they were co-workers as well turned out to be a very happy coincidence. "She's already begged me to ask Dom if he and the guys will consider a photo shoot called 'GI Joes of Danvers.' She's mentioned them wearing camouflage Speedos! Somehow, I don't think my man and his co-workers would want their other ex-military friends to see them that way."

"You're no fun." Mia pouted. "I've tried to get Seth and the Jackson brothers and cousins onboard because they are all absurdly hot, but he won't go for it."

"What'd I miss?" Suzy demanded as she sidled up with a tiny baby in her arms. Lydia tried her best not to stare, but it was hard. Suzy Merimon was a legend at Danvers. She was a beautiful and hip style icon. Lydia had always figured she could wear a burlap sack and still look like a million bucks. Today, though, she appeared a little frazzled. Her normally flawlessly styled red hair was hanging in a lopsided ponytail, and Lydia wasn't sure, but it looked almost as if her dress was on inside out. What stood out for Lydia, though, was the utter peace and happiness that seemed to radiate from her. And even as she stood bickering with her sister, she kept darting glances downward at the tiny bundle nestled so lovingly against her body.

Beth's lips curved into an affectionate smile as she stared at her sister. It was easy to see that she was thrilled that Suzy and Gray had finally created the family they'd wanted for so long through adoption. After suffering with infertility and miscarriages, it appeared that their prayers had at long last been answered. "I think you've got your clothing on the wrong way," Beth gently pointed out.

Suzy shrugged as if she couldn't care less, which appeared to amaze everyone in attendance. "Yeah, I know. We were just coming from the bedroom when John spit up again. So I cleaned and dried the spot and flipped the dress over instead of looking for a new one. No big deal, right?" she murmured absently as she stroked her son's cheek.

"Holy shit." Claire's sputtered exclamation shocked everyone. When Suzy turned toward her in question, Claire shook her head and grinned broadly at her best friend. "It's just that I've known you for so many years and you've always been so particular about your wardrobe. I mean you practically tossed Chrissy out of a moving car while yelling, 'Get her out of here, she's going to blow!' So this is a surreal moment for me. Let me enjoy it, for God's sake."

Suzy pointed toward the leather couches and chairs in the living room and motioned for everyone to follow her. "I'm not going to lie," she began as she settled on the edge of one of the sofas. "I got pissed on the other day, and I damn near lost it. I was full-on crying and gagging when Gray ran into the nursery thinking something dire had happened. When he finally put together what had happened, he started laughing. I was so angry, I threw a tube of baby butt cream at his head. And he just laughed harder. Then it rubbed off on me and I began giggling. Before long, we were both lying on the floor with our naked baby between us rolling around like loons. And I thought to myself, this is one of the happiest days of my life. I have baby pee on my face and probably in my mouth, but I don't care. I realized at that moment that it was okay not to be perfect. I don't have to look a certain way or be mother of the year. The only thing I need to focus on right now is my family and doing the best job that I can as Gray's wife and John's mother. Those are my two priorities. Everything else is just icing. So yes, I have puke on my dress, and it's ass-backward, but big deal. I'll probably have shit on it at some point tonight—although hopefully not my own."

There wasn't a dry eye in that living room when Lydia looked around to gauge everyone's reactions. To hear Suzy speak of the epiphany that she'd experienced had moved them all deeply. And every person there could take something away from her words. For Lydia, it was to find the joy in things that could well appear insane to others yet made perfect sense to her. The world might not understand why she was married to a man she hadn't even known a month ago, but right now, it brought her happiness, and in the end, wasn't that worth living in the moment for? She didn't know Suzy very well, but she found herself clearing her throat and saying, "That was amazing. And I think we'd all wear our entire wardrobes inside out daily to have that gorgeous baby you have. Congratulations to you and Gray. I'm so happy for you both."

"Hear, hear!" Mia seconded as she walked into the room balancing a tray of glasses and a bottle of champagne. "Hang on while I get the orange juice. This calls for mimosas, ladies!"

"And sex talk," Suzy added. "I might be a mother now, but I'm still the resident pervert around here." Pointing at Lydia and then Crystal, she added, "And you two need to catch me up. I haven't heard how the honeymoon was with DeStudo, nor have I gotten an update about Jake. I gather from the contented looks on both your faces that there's been a lot of banging going on. Let's start with you, Crystal. How was your tropical love fest?"

"Way to suck the romance right out of it, Suz." Beth sighed but looked vastly amused.

Suzy rocked back and forth gently with her son. She dropped a kiss onto the top of his head before snorting. "Nothing says love like being pushed up the sheets by a man." Winking at Crystal, she asked slyly, "Did Mr. Big live up to your expectations?" Lydia couldn't help giggling since she was the one who first compared Mark DeSanto to a young Chris Noth from *Sex and the City*. If the way Crystal was furiously blushing was any indication, her new husband definitely knew his way around a bedroom.

Surprising them all, Crystal said bluntly, "We barely came up for air the whole two weeks. I mean, that kind of surprised me considering we'd been all but living together since we met, but something about having the ring on our fingers and the Mr. and Mrs. titles . . . It made us crazy—"

"Horny?" Claire supplied helpfully then blushed. "I know exactly what you mean," she admitted. "Jason and I were all over each other on our honeymoon. I think it's the alpha male in them that gets turned on over feeling as if they own you somehow."

"Those were good times." Suzy grins. "You wife— me husband, cue the beating on the chest and all the other caveman tendencies. And you, Lydia? How's that hot piece treating you? If you tell me you're playing Scrabble every evening instead of crawling him like a tree, I'm going to flipping sob at the waste of such prime man candy."

"Well—we can't have you crying now, can we?" Lydia said coyly.

"I knew it!" Emma crowed. "There is no way a woman could be in the same house as a man like that and not do the deed."

"We certainly know you couldn't." Ava snickered playfully. "Plus, we wouldn't have to guess. You'd take out a billboard and tell us all about it."

Lydia found herself relaxing as everyone good-naturedly ribbed each other. She'd never had girl-friends she was close enough to share intimate details with, and something about it felt so right. As much as they all picked on each other, there was nothing mean or catty about it. These women would have each other's backs in a second, and she felt so fortunate to have found a sisterhood like that. "I'm just taking it one day at a time," she admitted when there was relative silence again. I have no idea if it will work out long term, but I'm enjoying the now very much."

Suzy studied her for a moment. "Well, you've already got the ring, honey. And something tells me you won't be giving that up." As Lydia studied the gorgeous diamond that Jake had insisted she not take off back in Vegas, she felt a stirring of hope. Could Suzy be right? Was it here to stay along with her new life with Jake?

If she had anything to say about it, she wasn't going anywhere other than home to her new husband at the end of every day.

Be careful what you wish for, Lydia thought wryly. She'd been home all of ten minutes from Suzy's baby shower when there was a knock at the door. Jake had called her earlier to say that it'd be at least seven before he got home as he and Mark were dealing with some labor problems at another DeSanto location. So she knew it was too early for him, and he certainly wouldn't be ringing the doorbell. When she looked through the peephole, she inwardly cringed as she saw Chris's frowning face. Lydia stood rooted to the spot, unsure if she should pretend that no one was home or take the opportunity to see what the other woman said without Jake home.

In the end, curiosity won out and she slowly twisted the deadbolt and opened the door to Jake's ex. "Good evening, Chris," she offered, trying to sound as if she wasn't insanely nervous.

"Where's Jake?" she asked as she tapped her foot impatiently.

"He's not home yet. He's going to be late tonight. Was there something I could help you with?" Lydia asked pleasantly, even though she wanted to close the door on Chris and her crappy attitude. *This is what I get for being curious.*

Chris brushed past her and swept into the house as if she owned it. When she reached the foyer, she spun around and snapped, "You think you're the queen of the manor now, don't you? Don't tell me you're buying into all those empty promises that men like Jake are so good at making. Trust me, that's how I ended up sleeping with him."

Lydia took a moment to close the door and regroup before turning around. She attempted to take the high road by saying soothingly, "I really don't think now is the time to discuss this, Chris. If you have issues with Jake, then you should call him and arrange a time to talk out your concerns."

"Stop patronizing me!" Chris hissed. "I'm not some empty-headed bimbo that you can speak to like a child."

At that moment, it became clear to Lydia that Chris was spoiling for a fight and wasn't about to leave until she'd gotten one. Never one to back down, Lydia straightened her spine and leveled the other woman with an unflinching stare. "I'll speak to you like an adult when you act like one. If you're going to stand there and continue to insult Jake and me, then you can just leave."

Lydia could tell from the tiny flinch that Chris had been unable to hide that she'd scored a direct hit. She had little time to enjoy it, though, before she was once again under verbal siege. "He's not going to stay with you. I mean look at you. Jake is completely out of your league. Regardless of his seeming confidence that he'll get joint custody of Casey, I think he panicked and married you. He figured he'd get me off his back if he were already taken and I'd just let it go. Of course, if that happens, he'll have no reason to keep you around. How long do you think you'll be Mrs. Hay then?"

Even though Chris's barbs were getting to her, Lydia refused to let her see the impact they were having. If the other woman sensed weakness, it would be all over. She'd go for the jugular. "Isn't this whole tirade because I'm married to the man you want? Haven't you been badgering him to marry you for months? But he wouldn't. Why do you think that is, Chris? He loves his daughter dearly, so how badly must he dislike you not to consider a move that would give him more permanence in Casey's life?" *Direct hit*, Lydia thought as the other woman's face paled. Lydia wanted to feel more pleasure in Chris's pain than she did. Possibly because she knew she might well be the next one devastated when she no longer had the right to be the woman of the house. Dropping her head, she sighed. "I shouldn't have said that. I don't want to fight with you. In the end, we all want the same thing and that's for Casey to be happy."

So the wrong thing to say, Lydia thought as Chris's face went from white to a vivid shade of red.

"You know nothing about my daughter! Jake would leave you in a second if I held Casey over his head. There's no way he would ever choose you over her!"

Lydia was fast losing her temper with the insane woman in front of her. She'd never been driven to violence against another person before, but she had to clench her fists at her sides to keep from wringing Chris's neck. "Casey shouldn't be a bargaining chip for any of us. She loves you both and wouldn't understand suddenly not being able to see her father. No matter how angry you are at him or how you feel about me, she doesn't deserve to be jerked away from a father who loves her more than anything."

Bracing for the attack, she was shocked when Chris shrugged her shoulders as if she'd suddenly lost interest in the argument that she'd started. "Whatever. I really don't have time for this. I need to pick Casey up from my parents' house."

As she made a beeline for the front door, Lydia said, "I'll have Jake call you."

"Don't bother." Chris snorted. "I don't have a problem finding him when I really need to. For that matter, he'll come to me when I snap my fingers. He always does." And that was her beautifully lobbed parting shot as she slammed out of the house. Lydia was almost certain she heard Chris chuckling as she walked away.

With her head still spinning, she went directly to the kitchen and took out the leftover wine from dinner last night. If there was ever a time that she needed a drink, it was now. She grabbed a glass and stood propped against the counter as she finished one off in record time. Then without pausing, she poured a refill but forced herself to sip it at a more leisurely pace. She wandered through the house and ended up in Jake's favorite recliner in the living room simply staring at the walls. She was still in that position when she heard keys rattle then the front door open and close.

Jake appeared before her a few minutes later looking too handsome for a man who had worked twelve-plus hours that day. He leaned down and ran a finger over her cheek before brushing a kiss across her lips. "Hey, sweetheart, how was your baby shower? Did you have fun with your friends?"

Lydia smiled wearily at him as he hunched down beside her. "It was amazing. Suzy is so happy and much more relaxed. Motherhood agrees with her in a major way. I'm thrilled to have Crystal home as well. Was Mark as giddy as she was after their honeymoon?"

Jake chuckled before taking the glass from her hand and pulling her to her feet. He relaxed backward onto the sofa cushions and tucked her into his side. "You wouldn't believe it. He was on cloud nine. Normally something as serious and costly as a labor dispute would have him chewing out everyone far and near. But he actually told the general manager in Boston that 'these things happen.' Hell, I don't know who was the most surprised by that. His assistant, Denny, literally lost it. I didn't think he'd ever stop laughing. I know it's a bit crude, but the term 'pussy-whipped' has been making the rounds among the men."

Punching his arm, Lydia giggled. "You're right, that is bad. I think it's wonderful to see two people so blissfully in love that everything else in their lives seems better. I don't believe there is much that could get to Crystal either at this point."

"Don't get me wrong, babe, Mark definitely needed to de-stress some and she's made that happen for him. When I first started with DeSanto, he was a control freak. He wanted to be in every place at once and handle even the smallest problem. But when she came into his life, that began to change. He no longer wanted to do all of the traveling or spend eighteen hours a day on the phone. He was finally able to delegate some of that to Denny and me. And even though Denny was perfectly happy being his driver and assistant, Mark has named him as co-vice president along with me. And I couldn't think of anyone more deserving. Plus, it gives me someone to split travel with, as well, giving me more time at home with my daughter and my wife."

Lydia felt like she'd been hit by a bus as his words sank in. He'd included her with Casey as if it were the most natural thing in the world. Did he really want to be in the position to be home more because she was here? She could detect humor and playfulness behind his statement. Going out on a limb, she replied, "I know Casey will be happy to have you around more. And even though you haven't been on a trip since we've been married, I'd certainly miss you if you were gone."

She let out a surprised squeak when he abruptly picked her up and resituated her on his lap. She ended up with her legs around his waist and her core pressed against his growing hardness. "That's better," he hissed as he took her lips. They kissed for what seemed like hours as he devoured her mouth. Her lips were swollen and tender by the time he pulled back enough to stare into her eyes. "I like hearing that you'd miss me, sweetheart, because I find that I can't get through the day now without wanting to see you. Knowing you're going to be here when I walk in that door at night does something to me that I never expected."

"And what's that?" she asked shyly.

"It makes me long for my wife. For the woman who has been sharing my bed and riding my cock every night."

Lydia started choking in shock at his raw, sensual words. He rubbed her gently on the back until she'd gathered her wits. "I like all of that," she admitted.

"That's real good, baby, because I need to be inside you now. I've been thinking about that perfect moment when my dick slides into your hot tightness all day. Trust me," he added wryly, "Mark isn't the only one walking around at the office with his little head doing the thinking instead of the one on his shoulders."

In what was an embarrassing display of enthusiasm, Lydia practically leaped from his lap and pulled her clothing off. When Jake could only stare at her naked form, she tugged him by the hand until he stood as well. Then she proceeded to help him undress until they both stood before each other completely naked.

She watched in confusion as he turned to toss a couple of throw pillows from the sofa onto the floor. "Should I sit there?" she asked as he moved closer to her.

"Put your knees on them, baby, and get down on all fours. I've been dying to take you from behind, and tonight, I'm going to do that." When she hesitated, he reached his hands around to grab her ass, kneading it firmly. "You'll love it, sweetheart. I'll be deeper than I've ever been."

She knew that he'd make it good for her; he always did. Jake never took his pleasure until she'd found hers at least twice. She couldn't imagine there being a more unselfish lover out there. He got down onto his knees next to her and helped her find the position that he wanted. When he was finished, her ass was in the air and her face rested on another pillow. He began caressing her backside, seemingly obsessed with it. Then without further warning, he slid a finger through the moisture that had gathered between her legs. "Ohhh, Jake," she moaned as her sex contracted from the sensation. He lazily circled her clit until she could hear the embarrassing sounds of how wet she was.

"You are so fucking beautiful, baby—absolute perfection." Finally, he stopped tormenting her and pushed one of his thick fingers into her channel. It felt different from this angle, more intense, and she knew she wouldn't last for long. When he slid the second finger inside and pushed deep, she came so quickly that she lunged forward in surprise. Jake caught her by the hips, keeping her upright until she'd found her balance once again. "I've gotta be inside you now. I'm going to go hard and fast. Let me know if it's too much and I'll slow down," he said raggedly.

She heard a rip and knew he was putting a condom on. She had no idea where he'd gotten it. Maybe he carried a stash all the time now. Then she could feel him there, pushing his wide tip against her slit. Without thinking, she rocked backward and gasped as she impaled herself on his big shaft. "Oh God!" she moaned. "It's too much, Jake."

"Shhh." He stroked her back soothingly. "Let me know when you're ready for me to move. I'll give you time to adjust, sweetheart." As she wiggled experimentally, she heard him take a ragged breath. The pressure was easing, and in its place was a hunger that she knew only he could extinguish.

"I'm ready," she whimpered as her need continued to grow. She gripped the pillow under her head and held on as Jake made some shallow thrusts before plunging deep. "Yes!" she cried out. Before long, they'd established a rhythm as she met him thrust for thrust. The sound of slapping flesh and their groans of bliss as they raced toward the peak together filled the room. When her knees began to wobble, Jake pulled her backward and wrapped one arm around her chest and the other hand went between her legs, rubbing her clit. After only a few strokes, she was screaming his name as she came around his cock. Her contractions pushed him over the edge, and with a harsh shout, he found his release as well.

After that, they were a leaden tangle of limbs on the floor for several minutes. Jake had pulled out of her and was now laying draped over her back as they both fought to quiet their breathing. She felt like a sated, but sweaty, mess. If she had any energy at all left in her body, she'd go clean up, but that wasn't an option right now. Since Jake was also damp and sticky, she figured they canceled each other out. "You okay?" he asked as he rubbed lazy circles on her thigh.

"Mmm, I'm great," she assured him as she enjoyed the afterglow closeness. Even though they'd been together for only a short time, he never treated her as if she didn't matter. He touched and kissed her for a long time after most sexual encounters. A few quickies hadn't left time for that, but otherwise, Jake liked to take his time with her. It was then that she recalled the earlier confrontation with Chris. She hated to ruin the moment, but she needed to tell him what had happened in case he wanted to do some type of damage control with the mother of his child. Clearing her throat, she said, "The reason I was inhaling a glass of wine when you came home was because Chris came by earlier under the pretense of talking to you."

She felt him stiffen behind her before he asked, "You think she actually wanted to see you?" She noticed he didn't seem surprised in the least by that.

"I think so, yes. She did ask where you were at first, but I got the feeling that wasn't the reason she stopped by. I think she wanted to feel me out and to let me know that she has the inside track with you."

"For fuck's sake," he bit out. "I knew things had been entirely too quiet on that front lately." He moved to lie on his back and pulled her to his chest. Cupping her cheek, he asked, "Did she upset you, sweetheart?"

"She made me a little angry, but nothing I couldn't handle. I think she knows or, at least, guesses that we married because of your concern for Casey. She mentioned it while she was telling me that you wouldn't have any use for me after she backed off on her threats."

"I'm actually surprised it took her this long to seek you out," he said, sounding exasperated. "And please don't take anything she said seriously. She's pissed that you have what she wanted. It's that simple. She doesn't care at all about the people involved."

Doing exactly the thing that Crystal had warned her against, Lydia found herself asking, "But do I really have that, Jake? You have to admit we haven't talked about what's going on between us and I'm a little confused about where we're going. Especially if Chris does back off and the threat of losing Casey isn't there for you." *What am I doing? Me and my big mouth!*

He studied her intently for a moment before asking, "Are you not happy with how things have been since you've been here?"

"What? No—I mean yes! It's been amazing. I love living here and being with you." *Crap, why did I toss out the love word?*

"I feel the same," he stunned her by admitting. "So please disregard Chris and her jealous rage."

"Okay," she whispered softly. It wasn't until she was dozing in bed later that she realized he'd never answered her question. Other than him admitting to enjoying their current situation, he'd made no promises or mentioned anything about the future. Had it been a mere oversight or had he ignored that part on purpose? She couldn't bring it up again anytime soon without looking like some kind of insecure clinger. For now, if she wanted to be with Jake, she would have to take each day as it came and hope he saw her as more than someone to warm his bed.

For the first time since she'd taken the plunge and moved in with him, she missed her old life. Sure, she'd only been half-alive, but her stress level had been so much lower. Really, when you had nothing left to lose, what was there to worry about? *Life as the neighborhood cat lady?* These days it felt like she suddenly had a lot on the line that she stood to lose.

Chapter Eight

I'm an asshole, Jake thought the next morning as he sat in his office at the Myrtle Beach DeSanto headquarters. He'd evaded Lydia's question about their future last night and had been relieved when she hadn't called him on it. Truthfully, he hadn't known what to say. He'd never expected to feel the array of confusing emotions that had come with becoming intimately involved with the woman who was legally his wife. Hell, even that word still turned him on. How powerful it felt to have one woman who belonged with you. Even if it was just on paper.

As much as it called to the alpha inside him, it confused the hell out of a guy who'd never spent much time in relationships. His career had always come first to him. It had been years since he'd had more than a casual relationship with a woman. Then in one crazy night, he'd gotten married to someone he barely knew. His wild attraction to the mixture of strength and innocence that shone so brightly from Lydia hadn't waned—in fact, it had only grown stronger the more time they spent together.

He felt like a coward now, though, for avoiding the relationship talk she'd wanted to have. He'd already picked up on the fact that she had a shy side, and it must have been tough for her to initiate something like that. It wasn't in a man's DNA to admit that he was clueless as to what was happening or where it was going. But that's exactly how he felt. He knew damn sure that he wasn't ready for it to be over, though. Possibly, it made him a selfish prick for wanting everything that she had to give him while not being able to give her any answers in return.

He was so mired in his thoughts that he almost jumped from his chair when a voice suddenly asked, "Everything running smoothly in Boston this morning?" He looked up to see Mark propped against the doorway, looking faintly amused. "You were a million miles away, weren't you, and I don't think it had anything to do with Boston."

For the first time in ages, he felt like a blushing schoolboy. When he was in the office, his mind was on work. He didn't sit around daydreaming about a woman. To get busted doing just that felt beyond strange. "It's nothing." He shrugged. "Just getting things straight in my head for the day."

He and Mark didn't really have a touchy-feely relationship; heck, most men didn't, so he was surprised when his boss came in and settled in a chair in front of his desk. "How are things going with the new wife?"

Quirking a brow, Jacob asked, "Shouldn't that be a

question for you to answer? You're the newlywed fresh from his honeymoon."

"I am," Mark agreed, looking supremely satisfied. "But you tied the knot more suddenly and under rather unusual circumstances. Frankly, I figured you'd have had the marriage annulled by now, or if necessary, been in the process of a divorce. But Crystal tells me that things are going well between you and Lydia. Which I knew anyway since you had no beef with Denny taking over much of the travel here. You once loved living out of a suitcase just as much as I did, so I'm thinking she's the difference for you."

"Are you saying I'm slacking on my job?" Jacob asked incredulously. "If Denny has complained—"

"Denny is as happy as a fat cat with an unlimited food supply," Mark cut in. "He's single and currently not seeing anyone so the travel is exciting to him. I'd hazard a guess to say it's the best part of his new job. You go above and beyond for me, so there are no worries there. I was simply making a point that you're content being in town more now, and I'm happy for you. I don't know Lydia that well, but Crystal has a very high opinion of her. Anyway, good luck with—"

Mark was getting to his feet when Jacob blurted out, "I have no idea what I'm doing."

The other man looked startled at his outburst before lowering himself back down and asking wryly, "I'm guessing we aren't talking about work since you can do that in your sleep."

"No." Jacob shook his head. "It's Lydia—my wife.

She's amazing with my daughter and I'm running home every day like a love-struck fool just to be around her for the evening. I swear to you, I almost asked her the other night if she wanted to do the crossword puzzle in the paper with me."

Obviously trying but failing to hide his smirk, Mark asked, "And that's a problem why?"

"I've never done a fucking puzzle before in my life, man. Have you?" Jacob demanded.

Chuckling, Mark said, "No, can't say as I have. But there's nothing wrong with it. It shows that you want to do whatever is necessary to spend time with your wife. People change when they get married. You find yourself doing stuff you wouldn't normally do. Hell, I bought my first box of tampons a couple of weeks ago. Walked straight into Walgreens, picked up the box, and dropped it on the counter like I was purchasing a case of large-size condoms. Then I grabbed the box before the kid could even bag it and ended up walking down four fucking aisles of traffic in the parking lot with them. So, yeah, your crossword dilemma doesn't exactly blow me away. It only gets worse, my friend. But I'm happy as a pig rolling in shit, so what the hell does it matter?"

Jacob burst out laughing at Mark's analogy. He couldn't imagine the uptight control freak that Mark DeSanto had always been admitting to buying tampons and being happy about it. Maybe his paranoia was ruining what could be something good between him and Lydia. He'd already married her so didn't he owe it to them both to give it a try? After only a few weeks, he couldn't imagine going back to his life without her—that had to say an awful lot about his feelings for her. Looking at his boss, and friend, he said sincerely, "Thank you for that. I'm a little worried about what you've done in the name of love so far, but hey, no judgment here, brother. I'm sure I'd do the same if Lydia really needed it. I'd damn well get that bag before I left the store, though."

Mark laughed, and then got back to his feet once more. "Oh, you'll do that and more, my friend. It will scare the total hell out of you at the lengths you're willing to go to for the woman you love. I was almost scared enough to pack up and run a few times, but luckily, I got my head on straight and realized I'd be throwing away the best thing to ever happen to me. Now, if we're finished discussing your feelings, how about we call Boston and chew some ass this morning? I'm afraid I've run out of nice where the damn manager is concerned there."

"It's about fucking time." Jacob grinned, glad not only to hear his boss sounding more like himself, but also grateful for the insight the other man had given him. He still didn't have a plan in place or much of an idea of where to go next, but the one thing he was damn certain of was that he didn't want his wife to go anywhere. If she was willing to grade him on a learning curve, then he wanted to give whatever was between them a chance to grow into more. As if he needed further convincing, it was nine in the morning and he couldn't wait to go home to see her again. Maybe he'd sneak up to her floor in a few hours to say hello. He wasn't sure who that would shock the most, though—him or her.

Lydia had stopped by Starbucks on the way into the office and picked up a coffee and muffins to celebrate Crystal's first day back at work. She was so excited to have her friend just across the hallway again. They took a few minutes to enjoy their breakfast while Lydia brought her up-to-date on everything that she'd missed business-wise while she was gone. Then she hadn't bothered to stop for a lunch break since she was still full from her earlier treat. So it was almost two in the afternoon when there was a knock on her door. Looking up, she was surprised to see Jake standing there looking incredibly hot in his charcoal gray suit. "Hi," she said softly. *That's my husband*, she thought dreamily. A quick check showed that he was indeed wearing his wedding band. She'd yet to see him without it, but it was good to know he wasn't leaving it in his desk drawer during the day. For a moment she had the desire to run up and down the hallways yelling that very fact at the top of her lungs. *Because that wouldn't seem insane at all.*

"Hey, yourself," he murmured as he walked straight over to where she was sitting and dropped a kiss onto her lips. "I was on my way back from a meeting with Jason and thought I'd stop by for a minute."

Beaming her approval, she said, "I'm so glad you did. How's your day going?" *Tone it down; don't scare him off by seeming too eager.*

"Better now," he thrilled her by admitting. Clearing

his throat, he shifted on his feet before asking, "Would you like to go out to dinner with me tonight?" Before she could answer, he shoved his hands in his pockets and began pacing her office. "I know we have dinner together most nights, but I haven't um . . . really taken you out on a date. Which is pretty shabby of me and I owe you an apology for that. You cook for us every evening and I'm not sure if I've even thanked you. I—"

"Jake," Lydia interrupted his adorable rambling before he could beat himself up further. "You always thank me and you usually clean the kitchen up as well. I'd love to go out with you tonight, but please believe that I've really enjoyed the routine we've developed at home. I haven't felt neglected or whatever it is that you're worried about. I believe we're both still adjusting to our um . . . marriage."

Appearing relieved, he gave her a bright smile. "That's good, sweetheart. I'm glad to hear you say that. So if you want to come home after work, we can change and go somewhere nice and relaxing. I'll take care of making the reservations. Is there any certain type of food that you prefer or don't like at all?"

"Why don't you surprise me," Lydia suggested playfully. She doubted she'd taste the food anyway with Jake sitting across from her.

Coming to her side once again, his voice dropped as he said, "I plan to do just that all evening." When he lifted her hair aside and pressed a kiss just below her ear, she thought she'd crawl out of her skin. "I'll see you at home, my beauty," he murmured before straightening and walking out the door.

Lydia sat there staring after him like some kind of sap, wondering if she'd somehow imagined the whole visit. They'd been having sex for weeks by this point, but this somehow felt different. His invitation and words had held a decidedly romantic tone. Maybe she'd gotten through to him last night, after all. He might not have wanted to have the relationship talk, but it appeared that he was letting her know without words that he wanted more than a fake marriage with benefits from her.

She spent the rest of the afternoon in giddy anticipation of her date. She was literally bouncing when she crossed the lobby of Danvers several hours later. She was walking through the revolving doors when she heard someone calling her name. She stopped abruptly in her tracks when she saw Brett's mother, Connie, standing a few feet away. It had been a while since she'd spoken to the other woman so having her appear as if out of thin air was more than a little shocking. Attempting to gather her composure, she approached the woman with whom she had once been so close. "Connie, what a nice surprise. Is everything okay?" she asked, concerned that something had happened to Brett's father or brother.

Connie reached out, touching Lydia's arm. "Honey, I've been worried about you. I've stopped by your apartment a few times, but you weren't there. And Mike and I changed cell phones last month and we didn't have your phone number programmed into the new ones. I finally decided to come and check on you myself. I just knew something had to be wrong for you to miss Brett's birthday. I thought maybe you'd gone without me, but there were no new flowers there and you always bring some."

Lydia was dimly aware that the other woman continued to talk, but it was impossible to focus on the words over the roaring in her head. *Oh my, God, I forgot him! I didn't visit Brett on his birthday.* Looking back, she was pretty sure she made some excuse to Connie about needing to be somewhere, but she wasn't positive. The only thing she knew was that she had to get away.

She had no idea how she got to her car, but suddenly, she was driving toward Rolling Green's Cemetery. Her stomach was churning and tears rolled relentlessly down her checks as the guilt threatened to suffocate her. Then a fresh wave of horror hit as she wondered if Connie had noticed the wedding ring on her finger. First, she'd missed Brett's birthday, and then, she hadn't even had the courtesy to tell the Morgans that she had gotten married. She and Jake might still be in the process of figuring what their relationship status would entail, but she still should have warned them. She didn't want them to hear about it from someone else. They'd be so hurt.

As she turned into the serene grounds that were Brett's final resting place, Lydia parked in the first space that she came to and flew out of the car. *I forgot the flowers*, she thought hysterically. But she didn't want to turn back now. She'd bring them back later. His tombstone was located near a gorgeous crape myrtle tree. The blooms were vibrant pink and attempted to bring cheer to an area that normally knew only sorrow. Lydia liked to think that he enjoyed the beautiful blooms that covered the area around his grave.

Her hands were shaking as she found a grassy spot next to his headstone and sat down, not caring if she ruined the dress she was wearing. "I'm so sorry I missed your birthday. So much is going on that you don't know about, but that's no excuse. Brett, you were the most important person in my life for so many years. We grew into the adults that we wanted to be together. And if not for cancer taking you away, we'd be married right now and possibly even have a family. But we didn't get that," she sobbed. "Instead, I've married a man I don't know to help him keep his daughter. I know that's not something you can understand because I've never been an impulsive person. But the night it happened, I was sad and so lonely. One of my best friends had gotten married and I kept thinking it should have been us. Jake—that's his name—was going through problems of his own. And we'd both had too much to drink. I ended up marrying him that night, and even though he tried to make it right, I've committed to staying with him and helping him keep his daughter. If you could see Casey, you'd understand that she's worth it. And Jake is a wonderful father to her."

Leaning her head sideways until it rested against the cold stone, she whimpered, "I shouldn't be telling you all of this. I was supposed to be your wife, not his. But not only were you my fiancé, you were also the best friend I have ever had. I've been so lost without you to share everything with. Even if you're disappointed or angry over what I've done, I hope a part of you will, at least, try to understand how alone I've felt since you left. As much as you tried to prepare me for a life without you, I still barely kept my head above water some days. Instead of living the way you wanted me to, I hid away thinking no one would understand or care what I was going through. And for a while, I was mad at others for being happy when I was so miserable. I didn't understand why they were given everything they wanted, and you were ripped away from me. One of my biggest mistakes was in hiding how I was feeling from my friends and family. They thought I was doing so well, but I wasn't. I went to work each day and said the right things then came home at night and curled into a ball of misery until it was time to do it all over again. I always had a ready excuse to avoid any socializing or interaction outside of my job. I did this for three years, Brett. Then Crystal Webber became my assistant at Danvers, and she was going through a divorce. I could tell the first time I looked into her face that she was dealing with a lot more than a broken marriage. So over the next few months, she and I bonded somewhat and I was finally doing small things like going to a movie or to dinner. I don't know if I've ever told her how much credit she deserves for breaking through the shell I'd constructed around myself."

Wiping her face with her sleeve, she continued, "As I began opening up to her, other parts of my life seemed to come alive as well. For the first time since you were gone, I was feeling something beyond grief again. I saw blue skies where there had only been gray. The world was slowly gaining some vibrancy, and even as I wanted to revel in it, I also felt guilt that you weren't here to experience it with me. It was a slow process, but I was starting to find myself again. Although I still didn't really know the me without you. Then one day, I met Jacob Hay when my car wouldn't start."

Laughing, Lydia looked up at the darkening sky. "I know you were always on me about car maintenance. But at least, that time, Jake was around and he took care of it for me. Nothing happened after that, though, before that night at the wedding. I mean I thought about him, but I didn't have the nerve to seek him out." She wondered if it would have been any different if she had followed up on their first meeting. Somehow, she thought not. In a way, it seemed as if they were destined to be the last two people sitting at the table that night, completely lost in their own misery.

Lydia thought she must be insane, but she felt as if she couldn't leave the cemetery without letting Brett know everything that was happening with Jake. She believed she owed him that much. He had encouraged her to find love again, although she had scoffed at the idea before his death. She hoped that if he could hear her words, maybe it would bring him peace to know that she was trying to do as he asked. She might have gone about the whole thing backward, but she was still putting herself out there and Jake was beginning to respond. "So today, Jake asked me out on a date and he was so adorably flustered while he was doing it. After my attempt at a relationship talk the previous night and his avoidance, I was quite surprised and thrilled that he came to me. But then I ran into your mother and she told me I'd missed your birthday and . . . I just lost it, Brett. It kills me to think of that day passing three days ago and, God, I'm so ashamed to say that I didn't notice. I don't know how long it would have taken me had your mother not found me." And with that confession, Lydia was once again sobbing. She felt that by forgetting such an important day, her memories of Brett were also slipping through her fingertips. Even sitting here now, she could no longer picture the curves of his face accurately. Was his jaw square? Rounded? Once, she could have drawn it from memory without a second's thought, but now, it was beginning to get fuzzy and that was enough to throw her into a panic. *I'm losing the last part of him that I had. Soon, he'll only be a shadow in my mind.*

Lydia had no idea how long she sat there alternating between talking and wallowing in her sorrow at the loss of her first love. Was this the way it was for everyone who'd ever lost someone before their time? You think you've finally moved on, and then something happens to shake your very foundation. In this case, it was realizing that she'd let a day that had once been so vitally important completely slip her mind. Dusk was beginning to fall as she made her way on leaden feet back to her car. Looking at her watch, she realized that she was already late for her date with Jake. Not that she was really in the mood for it now anyway. He was probably wondering where she was, though. She pulled her phone from her purse, but there were no missed calls. Shrugging her shoulders, she put her seatbelt on and drove toward Jake's house—or home as she'd come to think of it. Tonight, something about the whole scenario made her feel guilty. Maybe it was the weight of knowing she'd left Brett behind once again to find solace in Jake.

She was a few houses away when she spotted Chris's car sitting in the driveway behind Jake's truck. *You have got to be kidding me. What else do you have in store for me today, universe?* After parking on the other side of Jake's truck in the garage, she squared her shoulders and entered the house through the kitchen door as usual. She considered it a major stroke of luck that no one was in sight. She paused long enough to wash her hands and attempt to tame her hair as best she could. Her clothes were smeared with dirt stains from sitting on the ground at the cemetery for so long, but she couldn't do anything about it. There was no way she'd make it to the bedroom without someone seeing her. *Chris is going to enjoy this so much.*

Hearing voices from what seemed like the direction of the living room, Lydia moved quietly toward that part of the house until she was brought to an abrupt halt. The scene before her eyes was the absolute last thing that she needed on a night when she still felt so very raw. Casey was doing her best to show her parents the skills she'd recently picked up at her gymnastics class, which was adorable. What wasn't as adorable was Jake laughing with his daughter as Chris stood nestled against his side with her arm around his waist. *What in the hell?*

This was the last straw—she'd hit her limit for the

day. Backing out of the room quietly, she retraced her steps and was back in her car in less than a minute. She was absurdly grateful that she still had her apartment and that was where she planned to spend the night. When she arrived, she went straight to her bedroom and curled up in a ball on top of the bed. It appeared that the world was intent on giving Lydia Cross a giant kick in the ass, and she didn't plan to stay awake to see where the next hit came from.

Chapter Nine

It wasn't until Chris and Casey were leaving that Jake realized how late it had gotten. Lydia should have been home a couple of hours ago. Hell, they'd missed their dinner reservation as well. He'd been a little later than he'd planned getting home thanks to a last-minute conference call, so he had known they wouldn't have a ton of time before they had to leave. Then Chris had shown up unexpectedly before he'd even gotten into the house. He'd braced for a fight the minute he spotted her car, but surprisingly enough, she'd been the most pleasant he'd ever known her to be. According to her, Casey had insisted on coming by to show him the new moves she'd mastered in her gymnastics class. And as usual, where his daughter was concerned, he'd lost all track of time. He loved seeing her little brow furrow as she concentrated on something that looked a lot like rolling around on the floor to him but it was clearly so much more to her.

Now, he felt the first threads of unease because he had no idea where his wife was. She was always home before him in the evenings, so this was highly unusual. Pulling his phone from his pocket, he checked it for missed calls or texts and found nothing. He quickly pulled her number up in his contacts and waited anxiously while the other end rang and eventually went to voice mail. He left a message asking her to call him and let her know he was worried.

Then he paced restlessly for another ten minutes before calling Mark. When the other man answered, he got right to the point. "Could you ask Crystal if she's talked to Lydia this evening?"

Sounding instantly alert, Mark asked, "Is there some kind of problem?"

"I'm not sure," Jacob admitted as he ran a hand through his hair. "She never came home after work. We had dinner plans as well that I thought we were both looking forward to. Chris and Casey stopped by, so truthfully, I lost track of time until they left."

"Hang on," Mark said. Jacob could hear him questioning Crystal in the background before he came back on the line. "Crystal hasn't spoken to her since work. She said that Lydia was finishing some stuff when Crystal left, but she said she was leaving in a few minutes. She just tried calling her and said it was going to voice mail."

"Thanks." Jacob sighed. "I'm sure everything is fine. Maybe she got held up longer than she anticipated."

"Give us a call when you hear from her," Mark said, sounding concerned. Jacob assured him that he would and disconnected.

A half hour passed and by then he was beyond

worried. He was at the point of calling the police and every hospital in town when he decided to drive by her apartment. He'd only been there once, but he still remembered the location. In fifteen minutes, he was blowing out a breath in relief when he spotted her car parked in front of her unit. On the heels of that came anger. Why in the world had she come here without saying anything to him? Didn't she know that he'd be worried? She was hours late now and couldn't be bothered to make a simple phone call?

By the time he reached her door, he was pissed. Why would she suddenly after weeks of living together decide to come home on the day they'd decided to move forward with their relationship? If she'd had second thoughts, shouldn't she have at least had the courtesy to call him? Hell, even a text would have been better than nothing.

Filled with righteous indignation, he pushed the doorbell once, then a second and third time just to release some of his frustration. After what felt like hours, but was probably just several minutes, he heard someone moving in the apartment. He could imagine her looking out the peephole now, so he glared into the small circle. A *bit of an asshole move, but whatever.*

There was a click as the deadbolt disengaged and then he was staring at a very disheveled—and dirty?— Lydia. His anger was temporarily forgotten as he gawked at the normally immaculate woman before him. This was certainly a new side to her. He'd heard of letting your hair down or vegging out as forms of relaxation, but this look took that to a whole new level.

He found himself shifting uncomfortably on his feet as she stood there staring up at him. *Stop gawking and say something!* "Er . . . I was worried about you when you didn't come home." *God, I hope that's just mud on the front of her dress.*

Snorting, she turned around and walked off but left the door open in her wake. *After all these weeks together, I find out she's insane?* Jacob warily closed the door and followed behind her. It felt a bit like venturing into a rabbit hole, but he bravely soldiered on. When they reached her bedroom, she flipped on a light and he was disturbed to see that the dirt on her clothing also extended to her bed. By this point, he was beginning to have crazy thoughts that possibly his sweet wife was an ax murderer on the side. He was so intent on piecing together the puzzle that she presented that he almost missed her angry words. "You didn't look as if you were too concerned earlier with Chris glued to your side."

Come again?

Confused, he asked, "What are you talking about? I've been trying to figure out where you could possibly be for the last hour."

Pointing to the bedside clock, Lydia snapped, "Exactly! You didn't even notice that I was almost two hours late getting home, Jake. Didn't you think it would maybe take something major for me to miss our date? But when I get home, there you are with Chris looking as if you had no clue I even exist."

"Wait a minute," Jacob grappled to catch up. "You're saying you did come home, but you what—left when you saw that Chris and Casey were there?"

She put her hands on her hips looking equal parts irate and—hurt? He'd been so focused on her bizarre appearance that he'd almost missed that. In all honesty, he couldn't remember Chris being unusually close to him tonight. He'd recognized that she was more pleasant than usual, but like any guy, he just thanked his lucky stars when a normally bitchy woman was actually passably friendly. Hell, she could have probably humped his leg in the kitchen and he wouldn't have noticed. Chris simply wasn't on his radar in that way any longer.

Then the absolute worst thing for a man to face began to happen and he looked on helplessly as big tears rolled down Lydia's dirty cheeks. "I missed his birthday, and I never realized until his mother told me. Then I rushed there to be with him and to say I was sorry. I was so upset that I lost track of time. I needed you to hold me. But when I got home, I saw Chris's car. Then she was plastered all over you and you both looked so happy laughing at your daughter. I was the miserable outsider, and I couldn't take that. I was so mad at you when I left for not caring enough to wonder where I was. You didn't call to check on me when I was late. You didn't miss me at all. Now, standing here, I realize how stupid that all sounds because I'm just your rent-a-wife," she sobbed.

Fuck me, Jacob thought dazedly. First of all, he could barely make sense out of her statements. She'd talked so fast that the sentences had run together. *Whose birthday did she miss? Rent-a-wife? Shit!* A conversation like this was unchartered territory for him. He'd pretty much avoided and made a mess out of the relationship talk just twenty-four hours earlier. Now, his wife stood before him obviously needing some type of reassurance and an explanation as to why he'd made a fucking mess out of their first date night. And he hadn't a clue as to what to say or how to defend himself. Plus, he was still seriously lost on the first part of her explanation. With a sigh, he decided to do the same thing he would do for Casey when she started crying. He stepped forward and put his arm around her shaking shoulders before ushering her toward what he hoped was her bathroom and not the closet. "Shhh, let's get you cleaned up, sweetheart," he murmured against the top of her head. *Yep, definitely a twig in there*, he thought as something poked his lips.

He closed the lid on the toilet seat and motioned for her to sit there while he looked through a nearby cabinet until he found a washcloth. He watched her in the mirror above the sink while he ran enough water to thoroughly saturate the cloth. Then he returned to where she was waiting and dropped to a knee in front of her. She seemed riveted by his movements as he carefully cleaned first her face and then the slim line of her neck. She'd stopped crying by this point and now just looked drained. "Thank you," she whispered huskily as he made one last careful pass over her cheeks before tossing the rag in what he thought was her laundry basket.

Now to tackle the clothing. Where has she been? Even as he wondered, he didn't want to voice the question now that she'd stopped crying. She still appeared entirely too vulnerable, and he didn't want to say the wrong thing. Instead, he pulled her gently to her feet and located the zipper on the back of her dress. She offered no resistance as he removed her soiled clothing until she stood before him in nothing but a pair of tiny blue bikini panties and a matching bra. He grabbed another cloth and made quick work of giving her a sponge bath before wrapping her in a towel. She snuggled into his chest as he pulled her against him. "There, all better," he whispered. At that point, he knew he had two choices. Put her in his truck and take her home or change her bedding and stay here for the night. She was as docile as a child now, and he knew she would do whatever he wanted without argument. One thing was certain, though—he damn sure wasn't leaving her. In the end, she pointed out the location of her clean sheets and he remade the bed before stripping his clothes off and following her under the now clean linens. He took a second to grab his phone from where he'd left it on the bedside table and sent a quick text to Mark letting him know that he'd found Lydia and would talk to him tomorrow. He then moved closer to her and they settled in the center of the bed on their sides with him spooning her from behind—a position they normally slept in most nights now.

Jacob knew by the yawns that she was close to going to sleep and he'd already decided that they could talk about whatever the hell had happened tomorrow. So he was surprised to hear her speak in a voice that sounded close to alert. "I forgot Brett's birthday. Since he died, his mother and I have gone to visit his grave on that day. Only this year, I didn't call her to make the arrangements or even acknowledge it because it completely slipped my mind. She was waiting when I left the office this afternoon. She was worried that something had happened to me."

"So you went to the cemetery," Jacob guessed, although he still had no idea how she'd gotten so dirty there.

He felt her nod against his chest before she replied, "I did. I was so rattled that I couldn't think of anything else but getting there and apologizing." She paused before adding, "I'm sure you think that sounds strange since Brett is dead, but . . ."

Pulling her closer, Jacob said sincerely, "There isn't a right or a wrong way to grieve, sweetheart. He was the man who shared your life with you for so long. Of course, it would be upsetting to realize you'd forgotten something that you normally wouldn't have. But that doesn't mean you forget how much he meant to you. You're human, Lydia, like the rest of us. And you've had a lot of changes in your life recently. Don't beat yourself up that something got past you."

The room was silent for a while as she appeared to mull over his words. Either that or she'd fallen asleep. "I was hurt and jealous when I came home and saw you and Chris looking so cozy. I wasn't in a good place after visiting Brett's grave, and I guess I was expecting comfort and concern from you. When I found you laughing instead, seemingly without a care in the world, I ran. Which seems terribly childish right now, but at the time made perfect sense to me."

Jacob shifted her in his arms until they were face-to-face then he laid his lips upon hers. He kissed her slow and deep, taking languid sips of the sweet nectar of her distinctive taste until he felt his cock begin to take an interest in what was going on. *Down, boy.* This was about giving comfort, not sex. She'd had an emotionally devastating evening, and he wanted to hopefully show her through actions how much he'd come to care about her. Of course, his dick was more than willing to express its keen fondness as well, but he pushed his own urges aside to continue worshipping her soft lips. Finally, he pulled back to lay his forehead against hers. Both of them were breathing as if they'd just run a race, and he knew if he didn't stop now, he'd be inside her in another minute. "I'm sorry I lost track of time, sweetheart. But it certainly had nothing to do with anything romantic between Chris and me. This may make me sound like a jerk, but I couldn't even tell you where she was standing in relation to me any of the time that she was there. Casey had my complete attention. The only thing I did notice was that Chris was less disagreeable this time than she normally is. That's it—period. I was fixated on Casey's enthusiasm about her new gymnastics class, and I didn't realize how late it had gotten until they left. As soon as it occurred to me, I was worried and I began looking for you. When you check your phone again, you'll find missed calls and messages from me as well as Crystal. I called her when I couldn't locate you."

"Really—you did?" Lydia asked, sounding so relieved that he felt like an even bigger asshole. She'd lost her fiancé to cancer three years earlier and hadn't been involved with a man since then. Of course she would be uncertain in a new relationship in ideal circumstances. But considering how they'd ended up getting married, was it any wonder that she'd been so unsure of the fact he'd be concerned for her?

"Lydia, of course I immediately began hunting for you. And as far as the wife rental comment, I hope you don't really feel that way. I thought we decided earlier today that we were both ready to be a couple in the real sense of the word. Not that I'm saying that we haven't since we got married, but I'm committed to moving forward. I know that dealing with Chris is a lot to ask, and as Casey's mother, she isn't going away. Can you handle that?"

"Jake, of course," she answered without hesitation. "I know my actions earlier might lead you to believe otherwise, but I hope you'll understand that they really had very little to do with Chris and more to do with my being upset over Brett."

Rubbing her back soothingly, he said, "I understand. Just please don't do that again. If you need space, let me know you're coming here. And I promise I'll be more considerate in the future and more aware of what's going on around me. It's been so long since I've been involved with someone that I've possibly forgotten how to be that man."

Shocking him since she usually let him make the first move, Lydia dropped her hand and cupped his cock. He was still at half-mast from their kiss, and after only an embarrassingly few strokes, he was hard as steel. "I think you have a lot of potential to be just the man I need," she purred as she continued to stroke him through the boxer briefs he'd left on.

"Honey, I am trying to be nice tonight and let you get some rest after your rough evening. But if you keep doing that, my good intentions are going to be shot to hell."

"I think your cock is just the cure that I need," she murmured as her grip tightened.

Fucking hell, I tried, he thought as he moved to his back. His plan was to swing her over his hips and have her ride him. But Lydia seemed to have other ideas. She pushed his hands away and tugged his briefs down, releasing his heavy cock. She encircled his girth with one hand and began lightly, almost teasingly, pumping him. "Suck me, baby," he grunted out as his hips moved restlessly against her hold.

Clicking her tongue, she said, "All in good time, Jake." Then the minx proceeded to drive him halfway out of his mind with darting licks to his length while she massaged his balls. Just as he thought he couldn't take it anymore, she engulfed him in her mouth, letting him slide down the back of her throat. God in heaven, did she have no gag reflex? Then she swallowed around him and he lost it. Normally, he'd always warn a woman before coming in her mouth, but there simply wasn't time. He was shooting his load down her throat for what seemed like five fucking minutes. She eased him out some, probably so she could breathe again, but it had already been the best blowjob of his life. Apparently, she agreed because she hummed her approval while wrapping her lips tightly around the sensitive head of his cock. And sweet Christ, he shot another load into her mouth.

"Lydia! Baby, please . . . you're killing me!" he groaned, feeling light-headed by this point. He both wanted to leave his cock in her mouth forever and pull out before he passed out. Bliss, utter and complete, was what he felt. His wife—the woman who'd once told him she didn't have experience with oral sex—was a goddamn prodigy. A skill such as hers wasn't something you learned; she was born to suck cock—his cock. When she sat up beside him and licked her lips, he wondered if this was the one moment he'd remember forever. Had he really just fallen in love with his wife over a phenomenal blowjob? They said you know when it happens and he was half afraid this would be the story he'd never be able to relay to their kids. But he'd damn sure think about it again and again as a defining moment in their relationship.

Chapter Ten

Another month passed and Lydia was blissfully happy—with the exception of one thing. Or one person . . . Chris. The other woman had indeed changed her methods and was attempting to embody the *catch more flies with honey than with vinegar* approach. She'd had her lawyer withdraw her papers seeking sole custody of Casey and was doing everything possible to get into Jake's good graces. And dammit, Jake was oblivious to her latest tactics. Lydia was sitting at one of the picnic tables that were placed around Danvers headquarters for its employees, having lunch with Crystal. It was so nice outside today that they'd picked up some sandwiches and brought them here to eat away from the hustle and bustle of the midday crowd. Mia had to take a last-minute support call but planned to join them soon. "So how's life with Mr. Big treating you?" Lydia joked as she took a drink of her tea. She still thought of the character from *Sex in the City* whenever she saw Mark, and she didn't think that would ever change. She wasn't attracted to him at all in that way, but she could certainly appreciate the appeal of a rich and powerful man who was hot to boot.

"Mark is amazing," Crystal replied softly. "We just mesh so well." Lowering her voice, she added, "Our sex life always surprises me. After a few months, I would have expected that I'd know it all, but he's so—creative. Plus, he wants me all the time. Like even right after we've done it. Sometimes, we go again."

Lydia smiled at the incredulous tone of her friend's voice. Funnily enough, she could easily relate to what she was saying because Jake was the same way. He could and did spend hours touching every inch of her skin before going for round two. She found herself in a constant state of sexual awareness where he was concerned. Her body was so attuned to him that it was almost scary. One look or touch and her clit was throbbing and her panties wet. "I'm guessing you aren't complaining about his libido." Lydia giggled as Crystal blushed.

"Not in the least," Crystal agreed before adding, "but we both certainly had a buzz kill last night. We had our parents over for dinner."

"Yikes." Lydia cringed. She knew from Crystal how overbearing her mother was. Crystal had also told her about the struggles Mark's father had with addiction. She couldn't imagine it was a relaxing evening.

Shaking her head, Crystal said, "It was painful. Mark's parents were actually enjoyable. They're doing really well, and his dad is still hanging in there with his sobriety. My mother was a different story. She's tried to be better lately, but sometimes, that's met with varying degrees of success. Last night was not one of her better efforts. She kept referring to Mark as slick. As in, 'How much did this house set you back, slick?' Mark is really patient with her and doesn't appear to get offended, but it's embarrassing to me. It would be like some one-woman comedy show if most of her humor wasn't so insulting."

"I swear, doesn't anyone observe the lunch hour anymore?" called out a disgruntled voice from somewhere nearby. Both Lydia and Crystal swung around to see Mia stalking toward them. "The install my team did at Beach Villas last week went flawlessly. Trust me; you know how OCD I am that everything is in order. But their manager is driving me nuts! She is calling, like, ten times a day. 'I don't think my dial tone is working correctly.' Or, 'When I hit the button for the speakerphone, everyone in the room can hear my conversation.' Geez, of course they can. That's what a speaker does!" Lydia was dying laughing, and Crystal was holding her sides as their friend continued to give them crazy examples of the calls that she had been getting. "I'm telling you. There isn't enough support to help her out."

"But you're going over there after lunch, aren't you?" Lydia guessed. Regardless of how much Mia might complain, she'd never leave a customer hanging, no matter how silly the issue. It wasn't in her DNA to be anything less than perfect where her job was concerned.

Putting her hands on her hips, Mia glared before slumping down onto the bench beside Crystal.

"Dammit, you know I am. If nothing else, this is a challenge to my skill in training customers and my patience at not choking a pain in the ass." Taking the sandwich Lydia passed over, she asked, "What'd I miss? If you tell me it was the sex talk part, I'm going over there to stand in the street."

Crystal bumped shoulders with Mia as she said, "I was just filling Lydia in on my latest mother drama. I told you about it when you dropped by this morning. So you didn't miss anything."

Mia shook her head as she took a bite of her sandwich. "I'm sorry, Crys, but I swear your mother is a raving bitch most of the time. I don't know how you can still manage to spend time with her. And Mark must love you more than you imagined to tolerate her as well." In what sounded like some kind of demented town hall meeting, Mia asked, "Does anyone have anything else besides Psycho Sandy that they need to discuss?"

Lydia raised her hand and muttered, "Well, I have Homewrecker Chris if you'd like some variety. She's also the guest you never wanted to invite, but don't know how to get rid of."

Grimacing, Mia asked, "The baby mama? I thought she had gone all nice now. Is she back to her witchy ways again?"

"Oh no," Lydia said wryly, "she's still sweet as sugar, especially where Jake is concerned."

"But things are really good between you and Jake, right?" Crystal asked, looking confused.

"We're great." Lydia nodded. "But I know that Chris

is up to something. She's all gushing and accommodating to Jake, but I've caught the looks she gives me when she doesn't think that anyone notices."

"You think she's playing him," Mia guessed. "I swear men are so gullible where a conniving woman is concerned. It's like they want to believe that the female sex is sweet and pure and can't process it when that's not the case."

"That pretty much sums it up," Lydia confirmed. "I know she thinks if she continues to be nice, then he'll relax his guard further and she'll be in. She isn't above using Casey to accomplish that goal either, which sucks."

"Have you talked to Jake about it?" Crystal asked, looking concerned.

"I've brought it up a couple of times, but I just come off sounding like I'm jealous, which only makes her look better. He thinks she's accepted things as they are and he's not going to make any waves with her when she's not doing anything to cause trouble. He was sweet about it. He asked if she'd said or done anything to me that he'd missed, and I had nothing. Really, how would he respond if I said, 'She's looking at me funny, make her stop?' So instead, all I can do is grin and bear it while I suspect she's making a play for my husband."

"I love how easily you say that." Mia grinned. "For two people who got married in ass-backward fashion, you're one of the happiest couples that I know."

"Mark says that Jake always refers to you as his wife at the office," Crystal piped in. "Have either of you said the L-word yet?"

"That would be a no." Lydia sighed.

"Well, do you love him?" Mia asked bluntly. "Are you holding back waiting for him, or do you just not feel that way at this point?"

Running a hand through her hair, Lydia admitted, "I do—love him. I know it's fast and we haven't been together for that long. But I was halfway in love with him that first night we made love on his kitchen counter. Er . . . I didn't mean to say that," Lydia stuttered.

Mia whistled in a move that would make a sailor proud. "Now, that's what I'm talking about! We all need to talk about sex more—the kinky variety. I'd be happy to tell you about a few of my hotter moments with Seth if you give the deets on Mark and Jake."

"No!" Crystal quickly interjected. "I can hardly look Seth in the eyes now. I swear when he came up to congratulate us at our wedding, all I could think about was the fact that he has a monster pecker! And that's something no bride should be picturing about another man when the ink isn't even dry on her marriage license."

Wiggling her brows, Mia said, "Well, honey, it is huge. If it makes you feel any better, I thoroughly rode that baby all the way to the big O-town just hours after that."

Despite herself, Lydia couldn't contain her giggle. She certainly wasn't a woman of the world sexually by any means, but Crystal, who was married to a well-known playboy, looked so adorably flustered. No doubt, one of the qualities Mark loved about her. Even after being married once before him, she retained that innocence that men found so attractive. "Don't feel bad," she whispered to Crystal. "I was thinking the same thing when I saw Seth as well. We know way too much about the size of his equipment and how he uses it."

"Blah, blah." Mia shrugged. "I love that man of mine and I'm going to brag about him from time to time. He knows it and he's resigned to the fact. Hell, I'd hazard a guess that he likes thinking that all of my lady friends know what he's packing."

Since Mia was speaking so candidly of her relationship, Lydia decided to ask a question she'd often wondered about. "You and Seth have been together for a while. Any plans for wedded bliss in your future?"

Not looking in the least uncomfortable, Mia shook her head. "We've discussed it, of course, and Seth has let it be known that he wants that sooner rather than later. Underneath it all, he does have a traditional side that wants to settle down and produce some offspring. I also love how our lives are right now and selfishly am not ready to change that. So we're happily living together until we're ready to take the next step. I have no doubt in my mind that he is my future. I might admire other men, but Seth became it for me shortly after my mother bought him at that bachelor auction."

Lydia's mouth dropped open as she sputtered out, "Wait—what?"

Crystal laughed as she asked, "You never knew that? Mia actually met Seth while doing an installation at his Oceanix Resort. Then her mother decided to purchase him for her at a charity auction."

"It was actually for a date," Mia clarified. "And after a few bumps in the road, we've been together ever since. I freaking love the hell out of that man."

"Wow," Lydia muttered. "I think it's official, Crystal—you and Mark have had about the most normal courtship of us all. Mia bought her man, and I married mine in a drunken Vegas moment."

Crystal threw out her hand, fist bumping them both before saying, "Yep, I just puked on Mark's shoes and passed out in his arms. I'd consider that pretty traditional compared to you two."

After their laughter had died down, Mia looked at Lydia and asked, "So what do you plan to do about Chris? That homewrecker is totally after your man. If he's not catching on to that fact, then you need to really be on your game. Don't give her any opportunity to be alone with him."

"But I trust Jake," Lydia protested. It felt wrong to consider watching him like some cheating boyfriend. She didn't think he would ever do something like that to her, but she certainly wouldn't rule out Chris giving it her best try.

"Why haven't you told him how you feel about him?" Crystal asked. "I know it's hard especially if he hasn't said it yet, but someone has to be first, right?"

"I guess I'm just afraid of making things awkward. I know he cares about me because he's said that many times. And there are times when I think it goes beyond that . . . but I don't know. I never had to worry about this stuff with Brett. He said the words first and often. But with Jake, I'm constantly second-guessing myself.

He's very affectionate and the . . . sex is amazing. We also enjoy spending time together just doing mundane things like cooking or watching football."

"Those are great signs," Mia assured her. "If he were just in it for the sex, he wouldn't bother himself to do all of that other stuff. He obviously likes being with you in and out of the bedroom. Regardless of why you got married, you have something between you that is continuing to grow and evolve."

Crystal surprised them all by adding, "He's your man, so take a stand with Chris if you have to. I almost let my ex-husband drive a wedge between Mark and me. Your relationship is the most vulnerable when things are new and you are still learning about each other. Be protective of that and watch her. Jake may just be glad to have her off his back, but a leopard doesn't change its spots and she hasn't changed who she is overnight. Knowledge is power."

"You're right, both of you. I promise I will be on my guard." Straightening her spine, Lydia added, "I'm in love with Jacob Hay and I won't let her ruin it for me." With new resolve, Lydia walked back to her office with Crystal after saying good-bye to Mia in the elevator. She was going to tell Jake how she felt about him. She hadn't come this far to chicken out now. If she wanted to keep the new life she had made, then risking her pride was a small price to pay.

Jacob approached Chris's table at the country club warily. Their last lunch, where she went nearly postal, was still fresh in his mind. When she'd called earlier asking if they could get together to discuss Casey, he'd hesitated long seconds before finally agreeing. He also felt strange about meeting her without speaking to Lydia first. Even though she'd never been anything but understanding where Chris was concerned, he also knew that it bothered her when he spent time with his ex. And that was something he was sympathetic to. He didn't think he would handle it well if their positions were reversed and he constantly had Lydia's ex-boyfriend to contend with. Those thoughts made him feel a bit like an asshole, though, since Brett was dead and that possibility didn't exist.

Chris got to her feet and gave him a warm hug, followed by a kiss on the cheek. "Jake, thanks for meeting me." Then she ran an appreciative glance over him before adding, "You look handsome, as always." Before he could reply, she quickly inserted, "Casey looks more and more like you every day." As was always the case, when his daughter was brought up in conversation, he lost track of everything else. God, he loved that little girl so damn much. He waited for Chris to take her seat again, and then politely pushed her chair up to the table before sitting across from her.

He ignored her flattery and asked instead, "Have you ordered yet?"

"Of course not." She smiled. "I was waiting for you."

Their server walked up at that moment and Jacob quickly ordered both his drink and his food, not wanting to prolong the encounter any longer than necessary. Chris frowned, looking disgruntled, but finally requested the garden salad with dressing on the side, of course. Would it kill her to just drench that lettuce in ranch dressing for once? He didn't bother to suggest it; she'd probably pass out. Lydia didn't have her dressing put on the side. Hell, she even ate pasta. Actually, that was one of her favorite dishes. "So what can I do for you, Chris?" he asked warily as the server placed his glass of water on the table. He was still a bit traumatized from their last visit here, so he wanted to be prepared if she suddenly went ape-shit. *Wait—what was brushing against his leg under the table?* He glanced at her suspiciously, but her face gave nothing away. He was on the tall side and the table wasn't that big. It would be easy to accidentally touch each other in passing. So he shifted slightly until whatever had been pressed against him was gone.

"We have a daughter together, silly. Wouldn't it be easier if we were friends?" she asked brightly.

Beware! Minefield ahead, proceed with extreme caution, Jake thought as he processed her words. Friends—really? How was he supposed to answer that? He'd gotten used to battling about everything with the mother of his child. Did he enjoy it? No, not at all. Was it mostly predictable? Yeah, pretty much. Her behavior had done a complete one-eighty lately, and it had made life easier. Although he couldn't help thinking of the saying *Beware a wolf in sheep's clothing.* He hadn't bothered to look too far below the surface of the recent ease between the two of them, figuring the unpleasantness would fire back up again soon enough. When he caught her staring at him expectantly, he muttered, "Um, sure. I guess so." Then he attempted to steer the conversation back to their daughter by adding, "So how is Casey doing with the new classmate who was bothering her? Did you go ahead and talk to her teacher like I suggested?" Casey had complained to him and Lydia about a boy in her class who was knocking the pencils from her desk and being a nuisance in general. He figured the kid actually liked her because that was the usual expression of adoration at that age. He'd done the same thing to Maryanne Sullivan until she'd given him a right hook in the neither regions. Apparently, her father had taught his daughter early on how to deal with pushy boys.

"Yes, Jake, of course I did," she huffed impatiently before seeming to catch herself. "I handled that the next day and everything is fine." Before he could reply, she quickly interjected, "So how is your . . . live-in doing? Will she be staying with you much longer?"

Jacob's glass halted halfway to his mouth. "Are you talking about Lydia? My wife?"

Shrugging innocently, she said, "That's what I said, wasn't it? I'm just surprised that she's still there. Your women don't usually hang around this long."

Setting his drink down with a thud, Jacob took a moment to control his temper before saying, "I'm not going to discuss her with you. The only thing I'll say is that she's not going anywhere. She's not some casual hookup. We're married and I don't see that changing. Is that a problem for you?"

And the charming, docile persona kicked in right before his eyes. Reaching out to touch his arm, she said sweetly, "No, not at all, Jake. I think she's a really nice person and I hope you two will be very happy together."

She was saying all the right things, but Jacob didn't think she actually meant any of them. In their situation, it was probably to be expected. If she'd moved on and gotten married or been in a serious relationship, maybe things would have been different, but she'd done everything up to and including trying to force him into marriage to her. So it wasn't likely she would suddenly appoint herself as Lydia's fan club president. He knew that his wife had also had concerns about Chris's new and improved disposition. It was suspicious considering they still hadn't resolved the issue of joint custody. Something that Chris strangely hadn't mentioned lately. It was a slippery slope indeed to travel. He'd never allow Chris to be ugly to Lydia again. But he also had to maintain a halfway passable relationship with the mother of his child for Casey's sake. He'd just go ahead and admit that most men weren't really that good at straddling the fence in that way. "I appreciate that, Chris," he said diplomatically. "I know it's been an adjustment, but we'll all get there."

"That's one of the things I wanted to tell you." She smiled as she took a bite of her plain lettuce leaf. Yuck, was there any dressing on that greenery at all? "I've been seeing someone myself."

Jacob had a mouthful of hamburger when she dropped that bomb, and it damn near went down the wrong way. Out of all the things he'd expected her to say, that wasn't one of them. Not that it bothered him that she had a new man in her life—as long as it was someone who was good to his daughter. But to his knowledge, she hadn't been involved with anyone in quite some time. It might sound vain, but she'd spent most of the last few years trying to get him back into bed. He wasn't naïve enough to believe there hadn't been someone here and there, but she certainly kept it very quiet. Casey had never mentioned a new uncle appearing out of the blue or anything, and his daughter would have certainly told him all about it if Mom had a new boyfriend. When he finally managed to swallow his food, he said, "Well, good for you. Is it serious?"

She toyed with her hair, watching him carefully. "It's possible. His name is Dean and he's a plastic surgeon."

Impressed despite himself, he asked, "So we're talking face-lifts and such?"

She actually blushed—something he wouldn't have thought her capable of before motioning to her chest. "Er—breastaugmentation." She said it so fast that the entire thing came out as one word, but he knew he heard the breast part and couldn't control the chuckle that came out.

"Oh, grow up, Jake," she snapped as she rolled her eyes. "It's a very lucrative field and Dean has a busy practice."

"I'll bet." He smirked. Breast enlargements in a beach town were probably like money in the bank. Heck, even he felt the urge to meet Dean now. When she looked ready to have another one of the tantrums she'd thrown on their last visit here, he wiped the smile off his face and got it together. He'd rather not have his membership canceled when she threw her dry salad at him. "I'm just kidding, Chris. Congratulations. I hope everything works out. Maybe we can all go out to dinner soon."

"Sure," she sniffed. "I'll mention it to Dean. He stays really busy, though, so it could be a while before our schedule is free."

After that, they made small talk, mainly centered on their daughter. It was quite possibly the most pleasant hour he'd ever shared with Chris. He'd let his guard down until there came another slide of something against his inner thighs. This time, when he attempted to shift and close his legs, he felt what had to be her foot just inches from his crotch. Unless her legs had suddenly grown a helluva lot longer, that couldn't be an accident. She had to be stretching to reach that far. *Say something or let it go?* "You are aware that you have your foot in the vicinity of my dick, right?" he asked bluntly, and then lowered his voice when the teenager at the next table turned to stare. *Fuck, he's probably Facebooking this conversation right now.*

"Whoops, sorry about that," she purred. "My bad."

My bad? Really? What is she, fifteen? "Do you think maybe you could move it then?" he asked. Just when he thought that maybe she'd moved on, she'd started a game of footsie with his cock . . . and less than a minute after telling him all about Tits Man Dean?

Sliding his chair back slightly, he planted his palms on the table and prepared to have an uncomfortable talk with her. As if sensing that, she jumped to her feet in a move so fast, it left him blinking in surprise. "Would you look at the time? I have an appointment in thirty minutes across town." Hurrying to his side of the table, she dropped a kiss on his cheek and ran her hand over his shoulder as she buzzed past him.

"Hell's bells," he muttered to himself.

He was still trying to figure out what had just happened when the teenager at the next table turned around and gave him a thumbs-up. "Dude, that was totally hot. You're like my new hero. That chick was smokin' and she wanted to get all up on you." The kid was with an older man that he assumed was his father. Unfortunately for Jacob, he was on the phone and not paying any attention to their conversation. The teenager looked completely mystified as he asked, "Why'd you run her off? You got someone better on the line?"

Jacob pulled his wallet from his pocket and peeled off a stack of notes to take care of the bill with a generous tip. Finally, he looked at the kid and said, "I'm married."

Shrugging his thin shoulders, the teenager said, "So?"

Jacob laughed as he got to his feet. "Stay in school, kid," he tossed over his shoulder. "I have a feeling you're going to need a plan B in the future." *That backup plan would probably involve some type of porn empire*, Jacob thought wryly. Never underestimate the youth of today.

As he walked to his truck, he couldn't help wondering what the whole point of that lunch was. Chris had told him that she had a new man in her life, but he didn't really get the sense the information was the point of the meeting. Then there was the whole foot in his lap twice. She'd always been fairly upfront in the past when attempting to put the moves on him, so today felt strange. It was almost as if she was tossing a little of everything his way to get a reaction.

If he lived to be a thousand, women would still be a mystery to him. One that he'd love to solve, but feared that he'd never sleep again if he did.

Chapter Eleven

"Your father and I are back from your aunt's house. I haven't talked to you in a few weeks, so I thought I'd check in," her mother said. *Try a few months*, Lydia thought dryly as she listened to her mother drone on and on. As she was an only child, one would expect that she'd have a closer relationship with her parents, but that had never really been the case. Instead, she'd left for college and her visits home had grown farther and farther apart even though they lived only about an hour away. It wasn't that she was abused or anything along those lines. They just believed in parenting directly from a childcare book but without many nurturing feelings thrown in. Apparently, that would make her a more independent adult, which possibly they were right about. She certainly hadn't had any issues cutting the cord and striking out into the world on her own.

"That's great," she replied, proud of the amount of enthusiasm she'd managed to interject into her voice. "Did you guys have a good time?" While her mother went on about their trip to Tampa, Florida, Lydia's mind went to what had caused the ever-widening rift with her parents. They'd fully expected her to desert Brett when he became sick. And they were completely against her leaving her job and traveling with him. She could understand their fears about her financial security even though she'd assured them that Brett had insisted on covering the costs of the trip. He'd made good money working as a computer programmer and had always been one to save every extra penny. Plus, she had enough money in her own account to give her plenty of time to find another job when the time came. The stress of having to deal with their displeasure along with the knowledge that her fiancé was dying was almost more than she could bear. That was one time in her life she needed them to step up and just give her a hug. Maybe lie to her and say that everything would be all right. Instead, all she'd heard was how she was throwing away her future for a man who wouldn't be around much longer. It had been so callous and heartless. Since then, their once cordial relationship had been decidedly frosty. They had no idea she was even married. When Jake had asked her about them shortly after their hasty wedding, she'd made some excuse about them traveling and her speaking to them soon. She'd been embarrassed to say that they likely wouldn't care, and if they did, it wouldn't be anything positive.

When there was a lapse in the conversation, she blurted out, "So, great news! I got married a couple of months ago!" *What am I doing? Shouldn't I have saved this type of news for someone like the paperboy? Or my favorite cashier at the grocery store? Anyone who would actually be happy about it?* Jake walked in the door right as she did her big reveal. She desperately hoped that he'd continue on to the bedroom and change clothes as he normally did, but no such luck tonight. He propped against the counter watching her intently. He had to have heard what she'd said.

"Then your father had some bad fish at a restaurant one night and was so sick I thought he'd have to go to the emergency room. I told him to have the chicken, but of course, he didn't listen to me."

Unbelievable, Lydia thought. Had the woman heard a word she'd said? Catching sight of her frown, Jake gave her a questioning look, to which she simply shook her head. When her mother paused again, she quickly jumped in. "Did you catch the part about your only daughter getting married?"

Her mother gave what sounded like a long-suffering sigh before saying, "Is this where you say something about being married to Brett's memory? Because frankly, that's not healthy and I can't encourage that kind of delusion."

WHAT? Lydia had nothing to say for a full minute. She was still attempting to process what she'd heard when the phone was gently pulled from her hand. It was a testament to how rattled she was that she didn't object. She was relieved to hand it off. Let Jake be the one to hang it up; it saved her the effort. Then she heard, "This is Jacob Hay—your daughter's husband. Mrs. Cross, I presume?" Lydia began choking, and

Jake calmly patted her on the back before resuming his conversation. "Yes, that's correct. Lydia and I were married a little over two months ago." She saw him wince before he added, "I am absolutely gainfully employed. In what capacity? Um, I'm the vice president of The DeSanto Group." Then in a strained voiced, he asked, "Is it—no, we don't have trash trucks. The DeSanto part is actually the CEO, Mark DeSanto's last name. It's not fancy for sanitation. No, ma'am, I've never driven a garbage truck." Lydia couldn't help it; she flopped against the countertop laughing as the normally unflappable Jacob Hay struggled with the questions her mother was asking him.

"Just give me the phone back," she whispered, trying to show him some mercy. His eyes were so wide they looked as if they'd pop out at any moment.

He bravely waved her off and continued answering what sounded like a bunch of bizarre and absurd questions. "What do I wear to work every day? Normally a suit. Why am I repeating your questions?" He flushed after that one before saying, "I'm just trying to make sure I understand you correctly. No, ma'am, I've never been arrested, but I have had a couple of speeding tickets." His voice had taken on a high pitch as he said, "It wasn't in a fancy sports car. I drive a truck. No, ma'am, not a monster truck, just a regular Ford truck. I own my home. Er . . . I'd have to look at the last appraisal to tell you what the value is—there are no tax liens against it of any kind."

Lydia was nearly on the floor now. Jake was so adorably rattled, but he continued to hold the phone almost as if determined to see it through. "Hang up," she wheezed out as she held her sides. "You're just encouraging her."

"Yes, ma'am, I have a daughter. Well, of course I know who the mother is. It would be kind of hard not to, wouldn't it?" He laughed then abruptly stopped. "No, I absolutely believe that women are equal to men. Um . . . I've never thought about being the one to give birth. I wasn't married to her mother. I . . . it just didn't work out that way. No, this is my first marriage." His face paled as he strangled out, "I—believe in safety, yes. I have a physical every year and um . . . it's all been checked and I'm good."

"Oh, dear God!" Lydia got to her feet and yanked the phone away from Jake before he passed out. "Mother! Why in the world would you ask him all of that? Have you any idea how personal and inappropriate—"

"I think he'll do," her mother interrupted. "Bring him and the daughter over for lunch one Sunday. I've got to run. We're playing poker with the Crenshaws tonight, and I need to make a trip to the grocery store." Lydia sat there holding the phone long after the line had disconnected. *What just happened?* Had she just gotten approval from her mother for the first time ever? It was almost more than she could comprehend.

Finally, she placed her iPhone down in front of her and looked over at Jake. He shook his head before releasing a loud breath. "That's one of the most fucked-up conversations I've ever had and that's saying something. Did you hear all of that?" he asked incredulously.

"I gathered enough from your answers to figure most of it out." She giggled. "It looks like I married myself to a dude who drives a trash truck and has no idea who his baby mama is," she joked.

"You're going to pay for that," he threatened as he started edging toward her.

She backed away, still laughing. "Now, Jake . . . you're the one who grabbed the phone. You asked for everything you got."

"Oh, really?" he said mildly as if they were discussing the weather. Then he dove and she squealed as he chased her around the island in the kitchen. On the third lap, she thought she detected a gleam of desire in his eyes and intentionally slowed down. When he pounced the next time, she let him catch her. And shortly thereafter, she had her first encounter with kitchen floor sex. The ceramic tile was cold, but Jake's body was hot—so very hot.

Later that night, while they were lying in bed, Jacob told Lydia about his lunch with Chris. He'd been torn about it but didn't feel right keeping the information from her. That made him feel as if he had done something wrong and he didn't really believe he had. His wife went still in his arms when he relayed the part about her rubbing his leg twice with her foot. "You're angry, aren't you?" he asked, knowing the answer.

She nudged him onto his back so that she could turn and look down at him. She caught him by surprise when she asked, "Do I have the right to be jealous here, Jake?"

He reached over and turned on the bedside lamp, wanting to see her face. "What are you asking me? Why wouldn't you? We're married, aren't we?" *Shit, was he actually encouraging jealousy? That was a new one.*

She sat up against the headboard and all of his male instincts were screaming that "the talk" was imminent. "I still don't really know what we're doing here," she admitted. "I mean, I know we're married and we live together. We obviously have sex—a lot of it. But— ugh! I'm just going to say it, and if you freak out and run, then so be it." She squared her shoulders and looked directly into his eyes. "I'm in love with you Jake. I know we got married for all of the wrong reasons and we haven't been together that long, but that's how I feel."

He felt panic rising at her words. Love? He'd considered the possibility that he was falling for her a few times, especially after some of the intimate moments, but what was he supposed to do? Say it back to her now? She was looking at him warily, but dammit, there was hope there too; he could see it. "I . . ." When his phone suddenly blared, he dove for it like a lifeline. He didn't bother to look at the ID as he answered the call. When he heard Chris's hysterical voice on the other end, he jumped out of bed. "Fuck! Which hospital? I'm on my way." He was already throwing his clothes on before he finished speaking.

Lydia had sprung from the bed as well and was scrambling to his side. "What's happened?"

"Casey fell down the stairs. Chris said the fall knocked her out, but she did wake back up a few minutes later. She thinks her arm might be broken, something about the angle looking wrong." He was already on his way out of the bedroom while Lydia struggled to dress. "I've got to go, I'll call you." Not thinking of anything except getting to his daughter as fast as he possibly could, he didn't notice the look of hurt on Lydia's face as he hurried away.

Chapter Twelve

Lydia dropped back to sit on the edge of the bed, attempting to process what had just happened. She wanted to go to the hospital—but did he want her there? He certainly hadn't asked her to accompany him. *I'm being silly*, she scolded herself. "I love Casey and I need to see that she's okay. If I want Jake to treat me like his wife, then I need to act like one." Getting back to her feet, she quickly dressed then realized she didn't know which hospital they'd taken the little girl to. She did quick calculations in her head and determined that Grand Stand Memorial was the closest to Chris's house.

Within moments, she was backing her car out into the night and driving across town. Fifteen minutes later, she parked in the emergency entrance and rushed through the sliding doors to the information desk. She was relieved when the receptionist told her that Casey was indeed there. When Lydia explained that she was her stepmother, she was given the clearance to go to the family waiting room.

After a couple of wrong turns, she stepped into the room and immediately saw Jake standing in the corner with Chris huddled in his arms. Lydia's heart rate accelerated, and she felt slightly nauseous. But she tried to calm herself down by justifying the sight before her. *Their daughter is hurt. He's just comforting her.*

Jake spotted her over Chris's head and looked uncomfortable, which somehow made the whole situation worse in her mind. If he felt guilty, didn't that mean something? Clearing her throat, Lydia asked, "Have you heard anything yet?"

"Lydia, you didn't have to drive all the way here. I would have given you a call when we found out something," he said absently. And those words hurt her more than catching him hugging his ex. With just a few sentences, he had effectively made her feel like an outsider. As if she was in the way when she had shown up here out of concern for his daughter. Plus, how often did he actually call her by name? Normally, it was always some form of endearment.

No matter how she was reeling inside, she kept her face carefully expressionless. *Keep it together; this isn't about you.* "There's no way I could stay home not knowing what was going on. I love Casey too," she added defensively. She moved a few feet away and took a seat. There were a handful of people on the other side of the room, but they all appeared lost in their own thoughts. She picked up a magazine and began flipping the pages, even though she couldn't really make out any of the words on them.

The silence was oppressive and she was absurdly grateful when Jake pulled away from Chris and walked over to her. "Thanks for coming," he said softly. Not trusting her voice to be steady, she simply nodded. He settled in the chair next to hers and she tried not to notice how Chris immediately took the one on his other side and laid her head on his shoulder. He absently put an arm around the other woman but didn't say anything else.

Lydia had no idea how long they'd been there when the doctor finally came in to let them know that Casey had a slight concussion and had indeed fractured her arm. But otherwise, her scans were clear. Apparently, she'd told the nurse that she woke up thirsty and wanted some milk instead of the water that she had on her bedside table. The stairs were dark and she must have missed a step somewhere. The doctor said that two people could go back to see her and Lydia watched as Jake and Chris rushed out the door.

She must have nodded off while she waited for them to return because, sometime later, Jake was shaking her awake. "Wh-what? Is Casey okay?" she whispered as she struggled to her feet.

"Casey is fine," Jake murmured. "Why don't you let me take you home? I don't want you driving while you're sleepy. I'm going to stay at the hospital tonight, but there is no sense in you doing that."

Once again, Lydia felt like she was being pushed away. She didn't have any experience in dealing with something like this, so maybe she was overreacting.

Getting to her feet, she assured Jake that she was fine to drive. He promised to give her a call in the morning and kissed her cheek before she left.

When she got home, she was so tired that she fell into bed fully clothed. As her mind attempted to process the events of the evening, she wondered where things went from here. She'd told Jake that she loved him just hours earlier, and he'd looked as if he was on the verge of bolting right before he received the call from Chris. All in all, not the reaction you wanted when you expressed your feelings to your husband. It was glaringly obvious that he didn't feel the same way about her. Or if he did, he wasn't ready to admit it. Maybe feeling like an outsider tonight would have been easier to deal with had that not happened earlier. As she drifted off to sleep, she wondered how life could be cruel enough to give her two men in her life to love when the fates had no intention of letting her keep either of them.

Jacob stared at the ceiling as he held his daughter's uninjured small hand in his. Chris's parents had arrived about an hour ago, and he'd urged her to go home with them for the rest of the night. He'd been desperate for some space to decompress. He was still tied in knots over Casey's accident. In the scope of things, she'd been lucky. Her injuries could have been far worse. This was the first time that she'd had anything more serious than a scraped knee, and it was freaking him out a little. He'd done his best to remain calm through it all, though, because wasn't that what fathers were supposed to do? He had a feeling that after the danger was over, the men usually found a dark corner somewhere and suffered a minor nervous breakdown before regrouping. At least that was what he was doing right now.

As he looked at the tiny head on the pillow, his heart clenched painfully. He'd never really considered what it was to love someone so much you were terrified something would happen to them. That type of vulnerability, especially to a man, was almost debilitating. Then he thought of Lydia and what she must have felt every day after finding out about Brett's cancer. How had she had the courage to face each day knowing that she was going to lose him in the end? His respect for her grew even deeper as he tried to put himself in her shoes. She was truly a tower of strength and she'd tried to share that with him tonight, but he'd pushed her away.

He'd been struggling to control his emotions, what with Chris being a mess. Then Lydia had walked in and he'd been so fucking grateful to see her standing there—his calm in the middle of the storm. But instead of it making him stronger, he'd been horrified to discover that he was on the verge of tears. And at that moment, he couldn't imagine anything more embarrassing than breaking down right there in front of her, Chris, and the strangers in the waiting room. Men just didn't do that. Hell, he'd never seen his father cry a day in his life. He'd been coached from a young age that males were the backbone, the strength. His mother loved being taken care of in that way. He suspected it made her feel special. The only way Jacob had known how to deal with the sudden onset of emotion was to shut down. And that had been a lot easier to do with Lydia looking at him with those beautiful eyes, full of concern.

After they'd seen Casey, he'd all but insisted that she go home. He'd hurt her for the second time tonight; he knew that. First, he'd acted like a coward and an asshole when she'd told him she loved him, and then he'd excluded her from something she was very much a part of. He was making a mess of a relationship in his life that he so very much wanted to work. But a part of him was afraid to face how important Lydia had become to him in a very short amount of time.

Casey shifted in her sleep, pulling her hand out of his, and he had to fight the urge to grab it back. He resisted and settled back into his less than comfortable chair. He put his feet on the bedrail and laid his head back. Not exactly like being in his own bed, but it would have to do. He let his mind wander back to his earlier conversation with Lydia. *She loves me*, he thought. He waited for the anxiety to strike again—but it was strangely absent this time. Had it taken the fear of something horrible happening to the girl he'd thought was the only love of his life to make him see there were actually two of them now?

He'd been physically attracted to Lydia from the start of things. And even soon after they'd returned from Vegas, when she'd doggedly continued to mention getting a divorce, he'd pushed the subject away time and again. At that time, he was convinced he was doing it for his own gain, even though he'd been genuinely moved by her sorrow over the loss of her fiancé.

Now, he wasn't so sure. Chris had backed down from her threats even though he was still pursuing joint custody of Casey. The court system was so backlogged it would take some time for his case to be heard, but Chris knew that he fully intended to go through with it. Yet he had no desire to divorce his wife. Actually, he couldn't stand the thought of it.

Perhaps he wasn't ready to accept that he'd wanted her for his very own that night because he'd been captivated from their first meeting. He had been upset about Chris's demands, but he'd never been one to rush into big decisions without a lot of thought, and he was beginning to realize that he'd thrown his whole rulebook away with Lydia.

It might have been lust at first sight in that parking garage, but listening to her talk about losing her fiancé at the table in Vegas and seeing the tears well in those beautiful eyes had touched something deep inside him. He'd wanted to be the man to give her everything she longed to have. As crazy as it sounded, could he have loved her all along, from the very first night they shared? He damn sure couldn't bear the thought of losing her. Just thinking of coming home at the end of the day to an empty house again was unthinkable.

Running a hand over his face, he accepted what he should have already acknowledged. He was in love with his wife, and he no longer questioned whether or not he wanted their marriage to be temporary. Shit, he hadn't looked at another woman since he'd met her.

He'd put it down to a hectic work schedule and spending time with Casey, but that had certainly never slowed him down before. No, the simple fact was he hadn't wanted anyone else. A part of him had known from the start that she was it for him. The rest of him had just needed the time to catch up and the courage to admit the truth. *Son of a bitch, I love Lydia.*

With that revelation, everything seemed to fall into place for him, and he felt a peace he'd never known. He hadn't been looking for it nor expecting it, but wasn't that how the best things in life happened? He glanced at his daughter. She was one such surprise and had shown him that he had a capacity to love that he'd never imagined he could possess.

He reached for his phone, eager to speak to Lydia, and then realized it was after two in the morning. Didn't he owe her something better than a late-night phone call when he admitted the depth of his feelings for her? Tomorrow, when Chris arrived, he'd go home to his wife and ask her what she was doing for the rest of her life. He hoped that answer still included him.

Chapter Thirteen

Lydia wasn't sure what to do the next day. She awoke early that morning and Jake was still at the hospital. So she got ready for work as she normally would and ended up arriving at Danvers almost an hour ahead of schedule. She was preoccupied with Jake and thoughts of where if anywhere they went from here when she plowed right into someone. "Oh, sorry," she automatically said, then jumped in surprise as a hand settled on her arm.

"Good morning, Lydia. Looks like we're both early today." Mark smiled at her. "Crystal was just getting dressed when I left, so she won't be here for a bit."

There was something so charismatic about Mark even though she wasn't attracted to him. He was darkly handsome, with an infectious sense of energy that emanated from him. Shrugging, she said, "I decided to get a jump start on the day. I was worried about Casey and Jake, so I didn't sleep that well." Then the thought occurred to her that Jake might not have let Mark know what was going on yet. "Did Jake tell you that his daughter is in the hospital?" Her throat tightened just thinking of the beautiful child that she'd grown to love suffering the pain of a broken arm. She didn't care if Jake or Chris wanted her there. She was going to see Casey on her lunch hour.

"He called me earlier this morning." Mark nodded. "I understand she's doing much better, but I'm sure it scared the hell out of him at the time."

"It did," Lydia agreed. She didn't bother to add that she had no idea how things had gone the rest of the night since she was shown the door early on.

She was shocked when Mark pointed at a seating area in the corner and motioned her toward it. Curiosity had her taking a seat on the comfortable chair and looking at Mark expectedly. Mark sat across from her and crossed his legs before saying, "I've known Jake for a while now. And I'm just going to admit that I was rather taken aback when I heard that he'd gotten married in Vegas."

Giggling despite herself, Lydia said, "I think we all felt that way, including Jake and me. It wasn't exactly a normal evening in my life either."

"No, I don't imagine so." Mark chuckled. "I think what's been even more interesting, though, is how he's settled down since his marriage."

"Was he some kind of party animal before?" Lydia joked, only half kidding. She'd known that he probably wasn't short on women vying for his affections, but was there more that she wasn't aware of?

"I actually wasn't talking about his personal life," Mark interjected quickly. The look on his face told her that he didn't even want to go near that minefield. "I'm not sure if you're aware of it, but both Jake and I did a lot of traveling for The DeSanto Group until recent months. I began to slow down on that when I met Crystal, and Jake gladly stepped up and took over my share. Even though I know it was hard for him with a daughter, he still did it without complaint. He and I are similar in that we'd rather do something ourselves to make sure it's taken care of than to rely on others. Hence, why we traveled far more than should have been necessary."

Confused, Lydia said, "But we've been married for going on three months now, and other than day trips, he hasn't been anywhere."

"That's right," Mark agreed. "I promoted my cousin and assistant, Denny, and he's been handling the long-distance travel for us—a move that would have bothered Jake greatly at one time. But after his marriage, he fully supported and encouraged me in the decision."

Then the reason behind Jake's agreement hit Lydia and she leaned forward to explain it to Mark. "Casey's mother had been making things hard for Jake, so I'm sure he wanted to be in town more often to avoid additional problems going forward."

Mark drummed a finger on his knee as if debating something before finally saying, "I know about the issues with Chris. He loves his daughter, but he also wanted to come home to you every day. He's in love with you, or he wouldn't have given up something that he enjoys so much. There are very few things in this world that will slow down and change men such as us and that's the main one. If not for Crystal, I'd still be circling the globe, so trust me, I recognize the same affliction in someone else."

Lydia gaped at him in astonishment. "I—that can't be right. He doesn't—"

Rather than argue or attempt to reinforce his theory, Mark got to his feet and looked down at her one last time, saying simply, "He does." And with that, he walked off toward the elevators and left Lydia reeling. Having a discussion about her love life with Mark DeSanto was one of the strangest moments of her life. Why had he told her all of that? She'd professed her love for Jake last night, and he'd acted as if he wanted to bolt. That wasn't the reaction of a man in love. Whatever Jake's reasons for changing his routine at work, they couldn't have much to do with her.

Mark might know business, but she was certain he wasn't privy to the personal feelings of his employees. No, unfortunately Lydia knew much more about Jake's private life than Mark did these days—and she would soon need to decide if she was willing to settle for a life with affection, but no love.

Jacob's parents made it to the hospital before Chris. They had barely been speaking to him over his Vegas wedding, but when they'd found out that their granddaughter was in the hospital, all of that had been pushed to the side. His mother buzzed into the room, and as usual, she looked impossibly young for her age. "How's my baby?" she asked as she walked straight to Casey and smothered her with noisy kisses.

"I'm doing pretty good, Mom." Jacob smirked.

His father walked in a few steps behind and rolled his eyes. "Son, none of us exist when the bug over there is in the room."

Jacob laughed, acknowledging the truth of his father's words. As the one and only grandchild, Casey held center court in his parents' attention anytime she was around. Getting to his feet, he did the manly hug with his father and then crossed to his mother. She waggled a finger in his face saying, "I'm still mad at you." He heard his father chuckling behind him as she continued to scold him. "My firstborn gets married and we're not invited? I have a daughter-in-law I've never even met." Looking suddenly skeptical, she asked, "Are you sure you actually have a wife? This isn't some acting-out phase, is it?" Putting a hand on the side of his face, she studied him. "Have you been feeling okay? I've never heard you mention dating anyone, much less a woman named Lydia."

As if the name finally penetrated the cartoon-induced fog she was in, Casey squealed, "Lydie! She my friend, Grandma. She cuts the crust off my sandwich and we pets the fishes together. Mama called her a ramp, but I still ain't seen no skates yet," Casey added in the innocent way that only a child can.

His mother looked from Casey to him before muttering under her breath. "Well, I guess she does exist since my granddaughter seems to know her." Clasping her hands together and giving him a look that never failed to freeze him to his spot, she said, "Your father and I are staying overnight with you. I'll make dinner and we'll get to know your new wife. You don't have a problem with that, do you?"

"Um, no, Mom," he answered meekly. The timing wasn't great, even though he didn't want to tell his parents that. He needed to be alone with Lydia to discuss everything that had occurred the previous evening. It didn't look as if that was going to happen now. He'd call her later to warn her so that she didn't feel as if she was walking into an ambush. One thing was certain, though, if she stayed with him after the ass he'd made of himself in the last twenty-four hours, coupled with a surprise visit from the in-laws, then he'd damn sure know she loved him just as much as he loved her.

Chapter Fourteen

Frankly, Lydia was pissed off. Despite leaving him a couple of voice mails and a text message, she'd heard nothing from Jake all day. She'd been forced to resort to calling the hospital, only to find out that Casey had been discharged earlier. That left her with the afternoon to imagine him at Chris's house playing happy family with her. No doubt, the other woman was milking it for all it was worth. She'd been practically wrapped around him at the hospital last night. Today, she was probably sitting on his lap and making everything all about her as usual. She could almost hear it now. "Oh, Jake, this has been so hard on me. I barely slept last night. My bed was so lonely and I was terrified. I just don't know how I can continue to live alone after my scare." And the scenarios played on and on in her head. Her feelings had nothing to do with Casey and everything to do with her manipulative mother. Jake might not be able to see it, but Lydia certainly did.

She stewed over it all the way home. *What an inconsiderate jerk*, she thought as she navigated the busy rush-hour traffic. It was better that she find out what kind of man he was now. She could deal with many things, but treating her as if she didn't matter at all to him was just too much for her. And to think, she'd let herself indulge in the fantasy that he loved her as Mark had said. What a joke that was. Well, she'd had it. She'd be waiting when he got home and she planned to give him a piece of her mind. Then pack her clothes and go to her apartment. She'd talk to a lawyer tomorrow about a divorce and move on with her life.

When she reached their street and saw Jake's truck in the driveway, her anger came to a boil. She should be happy that he wasn't at Chris's house, but all she could think was he had no reason why he couldn't have taken her last call. She couldn't remember ever being this angry before, especially at a man. Brett had never done anything to draw her ire. He called when he said he would and usually checked in during the day to see how she was doing. He wouldn't have ignored her, brushed aside her words of love, nor made her feel as if she'd overstepped her bounds by coming to the hospital.

Lydia parked, then got out of the car and stalked toward the kitchen door. She opened it and got a thrill when it slammed behind her. And there he was, sitting at the bar looking as if he didn't have a care in the world. Wait—was he seriously drinking a margarita? Lydia didn't know why, but somehow that was the equivalent of pouring gasoline on a fire. "Hey, sweetheart, how was your day?" He smiled brightly at her.

Are you kidding me right now? Oh, hell no! In a move

that surprised her, Lydia narrowed her eyes and stepped forward to grab his drink. He gave her a questioning look, still not seeming to realize how close to getting his ass kicked he was. She shifted as if bringing the glass to her lips before abruptly dumping it onto his head at the last minute. "How was my day?" she parroted over his gasps as the cold liquid ran in rivulets down his face and dripped onto the floor. "Well, let's see. I dragged myself to the office at the butt crack of dawn this morning after having basically no sleep last night worrying about Casey and you. Then your boss pulls me aside to assure me of how much you love me, which I know can't possibly be true since you practically broke out in hives in front of me last night when I told you how I felt. But against my better judgment, I started buying into it." Gesturing wildly with her hands, she continued her epic rant. "I found myself thinking absurd things like maybe you're just shy, which is laughable when you're a self-admitted manwhore."

"A what?" Jake sounded strangled as he gaped at her.

So fired up she couldn't stop now even if she wanted to, she snapped, "You heard me, whipper zipper! You have a woman in every port. Love 'em and leave 'em. But silly me, I fell for you anyway. And I thought we had something good going. I mean sure, you shift around like your pants are full of bees when I try to have a relationship talk with you, but otherwise, it's smooth sailing. Plus, we certainly can't keep our hands off each other. I didn't figure there was any way you were seeing anyone else with us going at it like bunnies."

"Lydia." Jake glanced around wildly before looking back at her. "Honey, I need to tell you—"

She was determined to finish unloading, so ignoring his pleas, she said, "But the absolute suckiest thing you could have done was to leave me at the office all day without answering my calls or texts." She reached forward and poked a finger in his chest for emphasis. "I'm Casey's stepmother and your wife. But I had to call the freaking hospital to find out if she'd been released! I love that little girl, and it killed me to be pushed to the side when she was hurt." Tears filled her eyes as her emotions took a turn in the opposite direction. "Do you have any idea how that made me feel, Jake? I should have been there last night, and you damn sure should have kept me updated on her condition. If you cared about me at all, you would have wanted my comfort last night instead of Chris's! I swear I could just choke you," she finished weakly, suddenly exhausted.

"Well, it certainly sounds as if he needs a good butt kicking to me," said a voice somewhere behind her.

Lydia stiffened and then whirled around. "Who?"

At some point, Jake had grabbed a towel and was now wiping his face so his speech was muffled when he said, "Honey, these are my parents, Ada and Joe Hay." Looking past her shoulder, he added wryly, "Guys, this is my wife, Lydia."

Well, this couldn't possibly get worse. Utterly humiliated, she turned to face the couple standing near the stove. His mother was stirring a pot and his father looked as if he was seconds away from rolling on the floor in laughter. Jake's mother put a lid on the pot then wiped her hands on a dishcloth before coming to a stop in front of Lydia. The older woman surprised her by throwing her arms around Lydia and hugging her tightly. "Nice to meet you," Lydia squeaked out against her shoulder.

Ada Hay pulled back and Lydia didn't know whether to be horrified or relieved that she was grinning broadly. "I always knew that any woman who married one of my boys would need a backbone. They're both stubborn, but Jake is probably the worst."

Jake's father snickered while Jake called out, "Thanks a lot, Mom."

"Um, did you hear all of that?" Lydia asked, hoping to God that they'd just caught the last of it.

"My favorite part was the 'whipper zipper.'" Ada giggled. "Don't get me wrong, no mother wants to know that her son spreads it around town, but I have a feeling that won't be happening anymore." Then she fixed a glare on her son. "You haven't phoned your wife today? I won't even go into why you'd need to call her when she had every right to be there with you."

Jake fidgeted uncomfortably before admitting, "Chris broke my phone this morning, and I haven't had a chance to get another one yet."

His father looked at his wife and nodded. "I told you I heard something when we were taking Casey down for ice cream. Remember, I went back to get my hat but changed my mind when I heard Jake and Chris arguing. As I was walking off, I heard a crash but figured the boy could handle it."

Puzzled, Lydia asked, "Why would she break your phone?" Considering Chris had been acting like an angel lately, that seemed a little strange, even for her.

Sighing, he admitted, "Because I called her out on her behavior at lunch the other day. Incidentally, she also confessed that she doesn't have a boyfriend and she just wanted to make me jealous. So we had the talk where I told her that I loved my wife very much and she and I would never be anything but the mother and father of Casey. She got angry and my phone was sitting on the bedside table in the hospital room so she threw it on the floor and then stepped on it for good measure." Despite the angry words she'd hurled at him, he looked deeply apologetic as he said, "Things got crazy after that. Casey was released and I had to deal with Chris acting like an all-time bitch. But that's no excuse. I should have found a phone to call you."

Lydia barely heard the explanation about the phone. Her attention was focused on the words he'd spoken before that. He'd told Chris that he loved her. Did he mean it or was it just a way to get her to back off? As she was struggling with what to say, his mother cleared her throat. "Your father and I are going to run to the store. I need a few more things for dinner."

"What could you possibly have forgotten?" Joe asked, looking bewildered. "We damn near bought out the entire supermarket not an hour ago."

Ada gave a long-suffering groan before taking her husband's arm and pulling him toward the door. "Do you really want to stand around and listen to the details of your son's sex life? I'm as open-minded as the next person, but I'd still like to keep a few mysteries where my boys are concerned. Now, can we please go to Publix to wander around for a while?"

Clearly not bothered in the least by her chiding, Joe looked at first his son then Lydia. "Well, I guess we'll let you kids have some privacy now." Pointing at his son with a smirk, he added, "Good luck, whipper. You're probably gonna need it."

Lydia knew that her face must be in flames as his parents left. Dear Lord, the intimate details she'd spat out in front of them! And the manwhore part. That one was likely to haunt her forever—even if it was somewhat true. Okay, maybe he hadn't been that bad, but all indications would point to the fact he had been a little fast and loose with the women. "So . . . they seem nice," Lydia said lamely. The room was quiet for so long that finally Lydia couldn't stand it any longer. "Okay, I'm sorry for saying all of that in front of them."

Jake moved to the sink and wet some paper towels as he attempted to clean some of the sticky drink from his face and neck. "That's my fault. I should have called you. Some of this could have been avoided if I had," he stated calmly.

Now that her anger had died down, she was getting nervous and feeling the need to fill the silence. "I may have possibly taken the whole, um . . . sleeping around thing a tad too far as well. You did say that you usually didn't have relationships, so I did have some basis for it."

His stare pinned her in place as he said, "That's

correct. I haven't been one for serious involvement with women in the past. But I also haven't been a man who lowered my zipper anytime, anywhere. I do have some standards, Lydia."

This was getting more uncomfortable by the minute, and frankly, after doing nothing but obsessing over her relationship and worrying about Casey, she was too burned out to go through it again. If he wanted to be mad at her, then so be it. Throwing her hands up in the air, she said, "You know what? I can't do this right now. I've humiliated myself by throwing a hissy fit in front of my in-laws, which is completely unlike me. I've never had to force a man to have 'the talk,' but I seem to be doing that a lot as well. I'm turning into one of those needy, clingy women that I never understood." Refusing to look at him, she rubbed her eyes before adding, "I'm tired, Jake. Mentally, emotionally, and physically. I'm going to go lie down and hope when I wake up, this will all have been some bad dream. Please apologize to your parents for everything." With those parting words, she forced herself to put one foot in front of the other until she was in the bedroom. She debated leaving and going to her apartment, but she didn't have the energy. So instead, she curled up in the middle of the big bed and allowed her body to relax. Her last thought as she drifted off was that Jake hadn't come after her. It looked as if she'd left the last pieces of her marriage, along with her dignity, in the kitchen.

Jacob scratched his head and tried to process what had just happened. To say he'd been a bit blown away by first the margarita on his head, then the verbal slap down, would be an understatement. His wife, it seemed, was full of surprises. Of course, that was probably to be expected when you didn't actually spend much time learning about each other before the actual nuptials.

Naturally, he'd been a little discomfited to have his sexual past ridiculed right there in front of his parents. He couldn't imagine many men who wanted their mother to hear them called "whipper zipper." It also bothered him that Lydia thought so poorly of the choices he'd made. But he guessed he couldn't toss all the blame on her. They'd rushed into marriage for all of the wrong reasons and then sort of fell into a relationship. There hadn't been more than a handful of meaningful discussions between them concerning their past. Although, possibly, he was the one who hadn't felt the need to confide in her. Lydia had spoken in great detail about her love for Brett and those years of her life. She'd also given him insight into what it had been like for her since he'd passed away.

Other than talking about his daughter and some of the issues he had experienced with Chris, he hadn't been as forthcoming and that was on him. He certainly couldn't blame it on the fact that she wasn't interested because he knew she was. It mostly came down to the lame excuse that men tended to avoid uncomfortable subjects and that included their past history of dating and sex with other women.

He'd planned to talk to Lydia tonight and tell her how he felt. He hadn't been expecting the big scene in the kitchen, though, so he'd been temporarily thrown off. He knew one thing, though. He couldn't let her go to bed another night thinking he was a jerk who didn't care about her. So squaring his shoulders, he prepared to go talk to his wife. His wet clothes were still clinging to him, and he hoped that if she felt the urge to toss something over his head this time, it was at least just water. This sticky stuff was damned uncomfortable.

Chapter Fifteen

Jacob found her curled around his pillow in the middle of their bed. He took that as a good sign. At least she didn't have it in a stranglehold or, even worse, kicked to the floor. He liked to think it showed that a part of her still wanted to be near him, even in sleep. He flipped on the nearby lamp and took a seat beside her. Then he simply stared for a moment. His wife was truly a beautiful woman. He'd told her that before, but he didn't think she believed it. She wasn't a vain woman. She didn't wake up and run directly to the bathroom to put on her makeup. Instead, she usually stumbled to the coffeepot with her hair sticking up adorably. She'd grunt at him in passing as he filled his own cup. Neither of them was that big on verbal communication before they'd had their caffeine fix. On the weekends, when they had more time, Jacob liked waking them both up in more pleasurable ways—no cup required.

Somehow, without his really being aware of it, she had woven herself into the very fabric of his life. It was only now as he stood there watching her sleep that he realized he wouldn't ever want to wake up to a day that didn't include her. And it was past time that he told her that.

When she stirred in her sleep, he took the opportunity to lay a hand on her arm. "Lydia—sweetheart, can you wake up for a minute?" He grimaced at his choice of words. He certainly hoped she wanted to stay up for more than sixty seconds after he professed his love for her. She mumbled something under her breath, but her eyes remained closed. *Time to bring in the big guns.* He toed off his soggy shoes and climbed up beside her. His body weight caused her to shift onto her back and he took advantage of the momentum to move her the rest of the way into his arms. Then he lowered his head and began feathering kisses on her face. One on her upturned nose, then each eyelid, the apples of her cheeks, before finally touching his lips to hers.

He was gratified to hear her moan, "Mmm, Jake," as she sighed into his mouth. More than anything, he wanted to roll her warm and pliable body underneath his and lose himself in her. But with his parents coming back at some point, he didn't really relish them walking in on him having sex with his wife. He figured they'd been traumatized enough for one evening. So he pushed the need for her aside as best he could and kept his kisses teasing and light. After a few more, her eyes begin to twitch, and then finally open. "Jake . . . what's wrong?" she asked huskily as she struggled to get her bearings.

"Shhh, nothing, sweetheart," he answered as he stroked her hair soothingly. "I just wanted to talk for a bit. I didn't like how we left things in the kitchen."

"I'm sorry," she murmured as tears gathered in the corners of her eyes.

"Lydia," he murmured, feeling like all kinds of a jerk. He'd hurt her badly enough for her to fly into a rage earlier, and now she was apologizing for doing something that she pretty much had every right to do. It was a bit harsh, yes, but again, that was on him. "Honey, I've been an insensitive pig, and I admire you for calling me on it. The only defense I have is that I've never been in love before, and I didn't know how to deal with it. Hell, I'm not even sure I recognized it fully until last night. You came into my life so suddenly, and then, in a short amount of time, I couldn't imagine it without you. I should have told you that every single day. You made this house into a home not only for me but for my daughter as well. Casey recognized your place in our lives from the very first day, and I'm ashamed to say that I was slower to catch on."

"What are you saying?" she asked quietly once he paused for a moment.

Before he answered her question, he settled back against the headboard of the bed and picked her up again, shifting her until she was straddling his lap. He wanted them face-to-face so that she would have no reason to doubt his words. He needed her to see the sincerity and the love in his eyes. "I love you, Lydia Hay, so much that it scares the hell out of me. But at the same time, it makes me want to be the best man that I can be for you and for my daughter. I promise you that what happened yesterday at the hospital and today when I didn't call you will never occur again." When she opened her mouth to speak, he put his finger on it, wanting to get the rest of what he needed to say out. "It's not that I didn't want you there last night. I was so grateful when you walked in. Then in the next breath, I felt as if I was going to break down. So I panicked thinking that I was going to do something embarrassing like cry, instead of displaying the strength that both you and Chris needed. Which I realize now sounds insane," he added ruefully.

"Oh, Jake." She laughed softly against his chest. "Don't you see that's one of the best parts of having someone that you love? When you're weak, I can hold you up and vice versa. We're both going to have times when we stumble, but what matters at the end of the day is that we always have each other's backs against the world."

Unable to resist, he took her lips in a slow kiss that quickly threatened to get out of hand. Finally, he forced himself to pull back. Quirking a brow, he asked, "So . . . was there anything you wanted to tell me?"

She wrinkled her nose adorably before saying, "Um, I'm starving? When are your parents going to be back for dinner?"

Growling, he began tickling her body until she yelled, "Okay, okay, I love you, you big lug! Thank you for apologizing for not calling me today."

He chuckled, shaking his head. "Wow, so romantic, sweetheart. Your words are better than the finest poetry."

"Would you prefer whipper zipper?" She managed to keep a straight face then dissolved into a fit of laughter.

"You're going to pay for that at some point, you little minx," he threatened good-naturedly.

"Mmm, I'd like to make a deposit on that right now," she purred as she began kissing and licking down the sensitive skin on his neck. When her hand dropped into his lap and cupped his semihard cock, he had her on her back within seconds. They completely lost track of time and where they were as she wrapped her legs around his hips and he ground against her softness.

Jacob had his hand up her shirt, cupping one creamy mound, when he heard, "Dinner's ready, kids! Whatever you're doing needs to wait until later."

"Fuck," he bit out as he reluctantly rolled off his wife. "I swear, they haven't been here in months, and tonight, they just won't go away. Wouldn't you think any sane people would have gone to the store and never come back after what they'd just witnessed? But no, not them. They're probably hoping we'll break out in round two for their amusement," he grumbled as he straightened his clothing before helping her off the bed.

"Honey, it's fine." She laughed. "I'd actually like a chance to show them that I'm not the crazy woman they met earlier." Jacob froze, riveted by how amazing it felt to hear an endearment fall so naturally from her lips. "What?" she asked as he continued to stare at her like a sap. Damn, was this love thing tricky. It was as if the moment he acknowledged his feelings, he had finally allowed himself free rein to bask in all things Lydia. She could probably fart like a pack mule and he'd still be enchanted. *Okay, that might be pushing it a bit.*

He pulled her into the circle of his arms and dropped a kiss on her forehead, then another on the corner of her mouth. "Nothing, baby, just thinking about how good this feels—you and me here together with nothing between us. Well, other than these damn clothes and my parents," he grumbled.

Then a knock sounded on the door and they both jumped. "Son, did you hear your mother? She won't let me eat without you, so come on out and face the music," his dad yelled through the door. *Well, hell.*

Exasperated, he took Lydia's hand and opened the door to find his father standing there smirking. "Guess what, Dad," he called over his shoulder as he and Lydia walked ahead toward the kitchen. "Lydia and I are going to be coming to visit you guys a lot more in the future. And we don't plan to stay in a hotel. No, we want to continue this family bonding, so we'll use my old room, which is right across the hallway from your room. Just one big happy family now." Lydia chuckled at his side while his father mumbled things under his breath that Jacob hoped his wife couldn't decipher.

Amazingly enough, though, even with all of the interruptions, he wouldn't change a thing about this moment. He'd never seen this in his future when he looked ahead. An incredible woman by his side, surrounded by his family. As surreal as it was, it also felt so incredibly right. And in the back of his mind, he could almost see the caption, *Whipper zipper finds a mate*.

Ada was buzzing around the kitchen when they walked in. The other woman paused to take in the way that her son was clasping his wife's hand firmly within his own before giving a nod of satisfaction. "Glad to see you two used your time wisely." Glancing up at her son, she added, "I assume you groveled sufficiently and promised never to be such an ass again."

As a burst of surprised laughter flew from Lydia, Joe slapped Jacob on the back. "You'll learn, son. The secret to a happy life is always saying you're sorry even if you have no idea what you've done. She's always right and you're wrong. Bring flowers home in the evening just because you might have hurt her feelings in some way that you don't realize and never get too old to call her honey, baby, or sweetheart. You're already parents, and someday, you'll add more to the mix. It's important that you remember who you are as a couple along with being someone's mother and father. The moment you lose sight of that is the moment you've lost your way."

Complete and utter silence filled the room as everyone seemed moved by Joe's insight. Ada walked right up to him and laid a kiss on her husband's lips that had both Lydia and Jake averting their eyes. After that, both of Jake's parents hugged Lydia and officially welcomed her to the family. Ada had fixed pork chops, mashed potatoes, and fresh green beans for dinner so instead of using the bar as they normally did for their meals, Ada insisted they have dinner in the dining room.

Lydia was surprised at how comfortable she was with Ada and Joe and how much their acceptance meant to her. Considering she didn't have a close relationship with her own parents, it was wonderful to already feel like a member of the Hay family in more than name only. With a pang, she realized that she still hadn't told Brett's parents that she'd gotten married. She felt horrible that she'd waited this long. She would go see them over the weekend and pray that they understood. They'd always been so good to her, and to lose them would be like losing that last piece of Brett. She'd e-mailed Connie to apologize for rushing off when she'd seen her at the office, making up some excuse about a missed appointment. She hadn't been able to bring herself to admit that she'd forgotten Brett's birthday.

"You all right, sweetheart?" Jake asked, apparently having picked up on her emotional upheaval.

She put a hand under the table and lightly squeezed his leg in reassurance. "I'm fine, honey. Just thinking of a few things I need to take care of." When he gave her a smile filled with love, she knew that no matter what happened with the Morgans, she'd be okay because Jake would be here to offer comfort and support should she need it. She had a husband who loved her—and she had to think that Brett was happy for her.

His parents had taken pity on them and left shortly after dinner. They'd already reserved a hotel room and planned to stay in town overnight so they could see Casey tomorrow before they went home. Lydia had scolded him after they left because he'd damn near pushed them out the door. The look on their faces had said that they knew damn well why he wanted them gone. He loved them, but damn, cock-block much.

"God, baby, you feel so good!" Jacob groaned as Lydia moved under him.

"Mmm, Jake, you're driving me crazy," she moaned in response as she tried to get him to speed up. Even though it was taking everything he had to go slow, he planned to see it through. His body completely covered hers except for her legs, which were wrapped around his hips. His thrusts were shallow as he ground against her wet heat. He tangled his tongue with hers again and again as sweat began to run down his body.

Whether she knew it or not, emotions had always been involved when they'd been together intimately in the past. No matter how he'd try to pretend that it was just sex, it was more. He'd been making love to her from the very first time—but tonight was different. He'd never discussed feelings during the act, and it was unexpectedly heady and exciting. Moving his lips to the skin below her ear, he whispered, "Love you so much, baby."

Her body shuddered in response as her legs tightened around him, pushing him deeper. "Love you too, Jake," she cried out. Those words from her had him dangerously close to blowing his load before she found her release. He tried his best to disconnect the feelings in the big head from the little one while he thrust inside his wife, taking them both higher until he felt her clenching and releasing around him. "Yes, oh yes!" she moaned as she climaxed around his hard length.

A moment later, he reached his own peak as waves of bliss washed over him. After what was very likely the best sexual experience of his life, Jacob figured some men would curse themselves for missing out for this long by playing the field. But as he pulled Lydia's sated body closer, he knew that he'd been waiting for her all this time, even if he hadn't realized it back then.

Chapter Sixteen

Lydia had spent her first girls' only day on Saturday with Casey at the aquarium. She'd come to think of it as their place now. Jake had taken a short overnight trip out of town on Friday, and Lydia had been shocked when Chris had called her on Saturday morning to ask if she could watch Casey for the day. Jake had texted to warn her. Apparently, he'd told Chris that he refused to speak for her, and if she needed Lydia, then she would have to ask herself.

She had to admit she had an evil moment when she really wanted to make Chris squirm, but that would make her no better and she wasn't willing to drop to that level. So she'd had a rather strained phone conversation and had readily agreed to spend the day with the little munchkin. When she'd arrived to drop Casey off, Chris had looked as if she'd swallowed something particularly foul when Lydia bent down to pick up the little girl. The little girl had hurled herself into her arms. "Hey, baba," she laughed as she called Casey by Jake's nickname for her. One that Chris absolutely hated. "We're going to have so much fun today!" Chris had thanked her stiffly before leaving to meet some friends.

Lydia and Casey had spent hours at the aquarium before meeting Jake for dinner that evening. To the outside world, they looked exactly like what they were: a happy family.

Sunday, though, was a day that she'd both looked forward to and dreaded. She'd phoned Connie Morgan on Friday and asked if they could have lunch together on Sunday. Jake had offered to come with her, but Lydia hadn't felt that it would be right. She had no idea how Brett's parents would react to the fact she was married now and hadn't told them. It seemed cruel to parade Jake in front of them before they'd had time to come to terms with the news.

Lydia arrived about fifteen minutes early and sat in the quiet corner of the bistro nervously twisting her hands. She almost jumped out of her skin when her phone chimed with a text. She smiled softly when she saw that it was from Jake. Thinking of you, sweetheart. Love you. Everything will work out. It still amazed her how Jake had gone from denying his feelings to embracing them fully without missing a beat. He made her feel so cherished any time he showed his thoughtful side. Her hands were hovering over the screen to text him back when she heard footsteps pause in front of her. Connie stood there looking down at her affectionately. As much as Lydia cared for Brett's father, Mike, she was relieved to see that he hadn't come along. She needed this time with Connie. Lydia got to her feet and embraced the woman she'd once thought would be her mother-in-law.

"I'm so happy you called," Connie said warmly as they took their seats. They made small talk until after they'd both ordered their food.

When the server dropped off their drinks, Lydia took a sip of hers nervously before saying, "I've got some news to share. And I want to apologize for not letting you know sooner. It just—happened so fast." Lydia had no plans to tell the other woman that she'd gotten married in Vegas under questionable circumstances.

Connie took her completely by surprise as she laid a hand over hers and said, "You've met someone, haven't you? You're in love. I recognize that look in your eyes. I haven't seen it there since Brett died." No censure was noted in the other woman's voice, just a sad acceptance that was almost worse.

Lydia took her napkin from her lap and dabbed at the corners of her eyes. This was going to be even harder than she'd imagined. In a way, it would have almost been easier had Connie been angry. "I do have someone in my life now," Lydia agreed. *Spit it out!* "Er, I got married a few months ago." When Connie's mouth dropped open, Lydia hurried on. "It was really sudden. We didn't have a formal wedding. Then I didn't know how to tell you." *Because I was so wrapped up in my drama, I forgot everything else.* Lydia felt like the worst kind of person as she watched the woman who'd been like a mother to her try to process what she'd just heard. She'd dumped a margarita over Jake's head for being an insensitive asshole, and she certainly deserved the same treatment from Connie now. Heck, she'd even hand her the glass of tea to use.

"Wow," Connie murmured, "that's a lot to take in." Pointing across the table at Lydia, she added, "I don't need to ask if you're happy because it's there, even though you're nervous about my reaction."

Sighing, Lydia nodded. "I am very happy. It's been a bit of an adjustment because I never thought I'd feel this way again. He has a six-year-old daughter as well whom I adore. She lives with her mother, but we still see her a great deal."

"So he has been married before?" Connie asked without any sign of judgment.

Lydia shifted uncomfortably. "No, he and Chris were never involved in that way. It was—"

"A hookup kind of thing," Connie supplied helpfully. When Lydia gaped at her, Connie laughed. "I might be old, but I know how things are." After taking a sip of her own drink, she asked, "Do you get along well with this other woman?"

Shrugging, Lydia admitted, "It's been a bit strained. She had hopes of one day marrying Jake even though there was no real bond between them, and I think it's been hard for her to accept that it's not going to happen. She was angry when she found out we were married. But truthfully, I believe she is beginning to begrudgingly understand that even if I weren't around, they wouldn't have ended up together anyway. I have no doubt that she'll continue to be a pain in my butt at every turn, but for now, things are calmer. We'll never be best friends and I can live with that. We just have to find a way to coexist peacefully for Casey's sake."

Just when she'd begun to relax, Connie pulled the rug out from under her by saying, "That day I approached you at work, you'd forgotten Brett's birthday, hadn't you? You looked like you'd seen a ghost when I mentioned it."

Lydia lowered her head into her hands as she confessed, "I thought I would be sick. It was the first time in three years that I hadn't been obsessed by that date for weeks in advance. I was stunned to have missed it. I went straight to the cemetery and stayed for hours talking to him about everything that had been happening in my life."

There was a squeak as a chair moved, and then Lydia felt an arm around her shoulders. "I wasn't trying to make you feel bad by bringing it up. Actually, it just proves to me that you've moved on, and that's exactly how it should be, Lydia. Brett would want that and so do Mike and I. It's hard, God, I know that's true. I still see him in small ways every day." Clearing her throat, she admitted huskily, "For so long, I clung to you because it felt as if we still had a piece of him. I'm ashamed that I didn't encourage you to start living your life again earlier. I wasn't ready to lose you as well, though," she admitted in a rush.

Lydia looked at the other woman in amazement, "Connie—I . . . don't know what to say. I never felt like that. We both needed each other to survive. I don't know what I would have done without you and Mike, and I can only hope that I gave you a small piece of the comfort that you gave to me."

In the end, the lunch that she had been dreading turned out to be more freeing than she could have ever imagined. Even though Lydia knew it was hard in a way for the other woman to see her make a life with someone other than her son, she also was genuinely happy for Lydia and wished her nothing but the best. She'd promised to call her in the next week to make plans for them to meet Jake.

It would take time and some baby steps, but she was hopeful that they would become as fond of him as they were of her. Lydia certainly hadn't been able to resist Jake, and she didn't think the Morgans would be able to either. She would never forget Brett, but she had learned in these last months that she had room in her heart for more than one person and she planned to embrace that each and every day.

Chapter Seventeen

It seemed as if it had been months since the ladies of Danvers had gotten together for a meal. Claire had organized a dinner outing to celebrate Suzy's return from maternity leave. She'd actually been back for almost a month now, but this was the first date on which everyone's schedules meshed. Lydia walked the few blocks to the Mexican restaurant with Mia and Crystal. Claire, Suzy, and Beth were a few steps in front of them, and Ella, Emma, Gwen, and Ava were bringing up the rear. If the laughter floating through the air was any indication, all the women were in good spirits and ready to blow off some steam.

After they had been seated, Emma rubbed her hands together and said, "Brant and Mac are running a taxi service for us tonight, girls, so everyone is getting the fishbowl margarita. If any of you have a bun in the oven, speak up now. Otherwise, you're drinking some alcohol!"

She'd already placed the order for everyone's drinks when Suzy put both elbows on the table and said, "I can't believe I'm saying this, but no booze for me. I'm almost four months pregnant."

Silence. You could have heard a pin drop as everyone stared at her as if waiting for the punchline. Then Claire turned to her best friend and asked, "Really? You're pregnant?" When Suzy nodded, Claire snapped, "Well, you know I'm happy for you, but damn, what happened to the whole telling your BFF everything? I just thought you were stress eating."

As Suzy glared daggers at Claire over the "stress eating" comment, Beth elbowed Claire. "What are you pouting about? I'm her freaking sister and this is the first I've heard of it." Then her expression softened as she asked, "Four months? You made it out of the first trimester."

"Oh, for God's sake," Suzy groaned as she looked at the teary-eyed group before her. "Can we please not make a big deal out of this? No, we haven't told anyone yet. With all of the miscarriages we've had, we didn't want to jinx anything. We have plenty of time tomorrow to talk about it, but tonight, let's just do what we all do best. Talk dirty and insult each other. I've spent months covered in puke, poop, and piss. Tonight, I want to be an adult." Giving Claire a pointed look, she added, "I'm not going to forget that comment about me being a pig."

"Whoops." Claire giggled. "I was just a tad surprised at the way you inhaled your donut this morning and then grabbed the half-eaten one from my hand and finished it off too." Holding her hands up defensively, she added, "No judgment here. I gained fifty pounds when I was pregnant with Chrissy. I have no room to talk."

"My ass was the size of a freaking tanker truck," Gwen piped in.

"Oh, it was not," Ella muttered.

"Really?" Gwen looked at her friend. "Dominic picked me up to carry me over the threshold and had to see a chiropractor for a flipping month after that. He could barely get out of bed the next morning, and we all know the man is in shape."

"Excuse me!" Mia waved a hand. "Hold it right there." Staring Gwen down, she asked, "And why would Dominic be carrying you over the threshold? Unless I'm mistaken, that happens after you get married. But to my knowledge, you haven't made an honest man out of your baby daddy yet."

Once again, silence descended. Lydia found herself munching on the chips in front of her as if they were popcorn at a movie. This was better than anything she'd seen in the theater lately. "Holy crap," Crystal whispered from beside her. She noticed her friend was also eating while watching the action.

Gwen's mouth opened and closed a few times before she released an audible breath. "All right, Dominic and I are married. There—cat's out of the bag. We went to city hall, so don't be offended. We didn't invite anyone."

"And when was this?" Crystal asked, sounding more curious than offended that she hadn't known.

"Afewmonthsbeforethebabywasborn," Gwen mumbled quickly before taking a big drink of her margarita.

As Lydia was trying to decipher what she'd said, Ava blurted out, "You've been married since before Cameron was born? That was months ago! Does Mac know?"

Shaking her head, Gwen said sheepishly, "No. I know those guys tell each other most everything, but we agreed to keep it to ourselves for now."

"But why?" Emma asked, sounding puzzled. "You have a baby together and you're crazy about each other. Why the secret wedding?"

"It didn't really start out that way," Gwen replied. "I've felt married to Dom since the day we told each other how we felt. We had so much going on trying to get a bigger place before the baby was born and preparing for his arrival that I couldn't take on anything else. Then Dom told me one evening that he really wanted for us to be married before Cameron was born. I had no idea that it bothered him. So we got our marriage license the next day and went to the courthouse to make it official. We planned to have a big party and announce it then, but um . . . we're still planning that party."

"That's a little whacked," Emma inserted but softened the sting by laughing. "You ladies can rest assured, when I marry my stud, you'll all know well ahead of time and you better damn well be there. I'm going to pick out some of the ugliest bridesmaids dresses you've ever seen and you're all wearing them." Pointing at Ava, she added, "You'll be getting the bubblegum pink one with all the lace as my matron of honor."

Ava, who was always impeccably dressed, visibly shuddered. "I guess I just assumed you'd plan something like a hog roast where you and my brother would wear overalls and grab each other's crotches as you said, 'I do.'"

The first margarita spray of the evening occurred when Ella spewed hers all over the table, and then begin frantically attempting to wipe it up. "Um, sorry about that," she muttered. Then she slid her hand across to give Ava a high five. "Man, that was a good one."

Even Emma, who had been the subject of the joke, couldn't contain her laughter. "I don't know about the hog part," she gasped out, "but I'll certainly have a handful of some part of Brant. I mean, Ava, have you actually stopped to look at your brothers?" Nodding at Ella, she added, "Chuckles over there is married to a man with that brooding, intense thing going on. And now, more often than not, he's carrying his daughter around, which is holy freaking hot."

Ella raised her glass saying, "Hear, hear!"

"Damn, I've missed you crazy bitches," Suzy muttered contently. Far from offending anyone, her comment was received by the entire group like a compliment. To be appreciated and accepted by Suzy Merimon was no small thing. She was outspoken and never bothered to temper her words for anyone. She would always be the coolest kid on the playground. The one all the other kids would gravitate toward and hope to become a part of her inner circle.

"I know we're not supposed to mention it, but how's the pregnancy treating you?" Beth asked her sister.

"Please don't throw anything at me!" She ducked playfully before grinning at Suzy.

Suzy rolled her eyes as if she'd been expecting the question. "Well, you know that whole pregnancy glow thing?" When everyone nodded, she deadpanned, "It's actually just gas."

"Ugh!" Mia gagged. "Women aren't supposed to admit to stuff like that. It totally kills our mysterious allure."

"Wait until you have a kid lodged up in there," Suzy warned. "I spent the first three months scared out of my mind that I'd miscarry, but this last month, I've relaxed enough that all of the gross stuff is finally getting through to me. For a while, something as simple as a gas pain sent me into a damn panic attack. Now I know I need to find some private place away from Gray and let 'er rip."

Claire, Beth, and Gwen were laughing so hard, Lydia was afraid they would fall out of their chairs at any moment. Having children themselves, apparently they understood where Suzy was coming from. Claire even managed to choke out, "Boy, do I remember that. Jason and I hadn't been together that long and then I was pregnant. So stuff like that really embarrassed me. The few times it slipped out, he'd be all cool about it, but I just knew he was thinking to himself, 'Steer clear of her tonight!'"

"Yeah, it's kind of a tough combination with the whole horniness so you're panting after anything with a pecker," Beth added. "I'd be wrestling Nick to the floor and have my hand in his pants before—"

"Must we talk about my brother-in-law?" Suzy gagged. "I've been lucky enough to avoid a lot of morning sickness, but you're making me want to hurl."

"I'm pretty sure that Dominic thought that was the best part of my pregnancy," Gwen piped in. "Even when I felt as big as a house, I still drooled when he walked into a room."

"Honey, everyone has a little saliva overload when he's around." Emma winked.

"Anyway," Suzy continued, "there's the gas, and yes, as you've said, I've been as horny as a whore at an all-girls' school." When a wave of laughter met her last statement, she shook her head and said, "You all really need to get out more. So, as I was saying, my tits hurt, it takes me like ten attempts to go poop, but I can pee every other minute. Everything I eat gives me heartburn, and I want to eat all the damn time. I made Gray go through the McDonald's drive-thru last night so I could have a freaking snack on the way to dinner. I actually ate a cheeseburger before we got to the restaurant for our actual meal. And probably one of the weirdest things is I love to smell car exhaust now. No shit, I'll be at a red light behind a big old monster truck and those fumes will be like flipping nirvana." Shaking her head, she added, "That's completely whacked."

"Wait until you get a case of hemorrhoids." Claire grinned. "That's when the real fun begins."

"Oh, hell no," Suzy huffed out. "There is nothing else weird going on with this ass. I'm already at capacity for crazy stuff right now." Groaning, she looked around the table and demanded, "Someone talk intercourse, please. I've never even enjoyed a good fart joke, so this stuff is killing me."

Lydia couldn't believe her ears when Crystal spoke up. "Mark spanked me last night, and it was so hot. He put me right over his lap."

"And that was so not what I was expecting to hear," Suzy said in disbelief. "It's way more than I could have hoped for, though. Boy, you don't play around, do you, Tinkerbelle?"

"Spanked by DeStudo," Mia purred, "how poetic. I bet that man gives excellent hand."

"Well, we don't call him Mr. Big for nothing now, do we?" Lydia joked. Heck, hearing that from Crystal made her want to go home and ask Jake to put her over his knee. She had a feeling he'd really be into that. He certainly was a fan of changing positions multiple times during sex. This one would probably blow his mind if she suggested it—when she suggested it.

All too soon, several hours had passed and Brant walked in, followed by Mac. Then surprisingly enough, Jake appeared next and headed straight for her. "Hey, baby," he whispered in her ear as he leaned down to drop a kiss on her upturned mouth.

"I didn't know you were coming." She smiled as she took in her sexy husband in his jeans and a T-shirt. The things she wanted to do to that man of hers tonight. She wasn't sure if they'd actually get out of the parking lot before she had her way with him.

"I wanted to take care of my own woman," he said possessively, which effectively set her clit on fire.

Jumping to her feet, then swaying slightly as the

alcohol hit her, she whisper-shouted to her friends, "I've got to go now." When Jake turned his back to say something to Brant, Lydia made a grabbing motion at his ass, causing the other women to howl in laughter. He flipped back around and gave her a questioning look, to which she replied innocently, "They're drunk."

Next to her, Emma appeared to be attempting a tonsillectomy on Brant, much to Ava's disgust. Lydia had a feeling it was also mostly for Ava's benefit. Those two certainly loved getting to each other.

Jake held her hand while she made her way around the room to hug each woman good night. Then he walked her to his truck and helped her carefully inside as if she were a breakable heirloom. When he clipped her seatbelt in place, she kissed his cheek before he could pull back. "I love you," she murmured dreamily.

His answering smile was soft as he replied, "I love you too, baby. Let's get you home and in bed."

"Mmm, I'm going to do stuff to you when we get there." Wrinkling her forehead in deep thought, she added, "I'm not sure what, but it'll come to me."

She heard him laughing as he shut her door and walked around to his side. He held her hand as they made the trip home. "It looked like you ladies had a great time," he remarked in a voice filled with amusement.

"Oh, we did." She giggled. "One of them is pregnant. It's Beth. No, wait, that's not right. Maybe it's Claire. And she has glow gas. Like really bad." Attempting to bring Jake into focus through her suddenly blurry eyes, she asked, "Would you still love me if I farted like a mule? Because someone at dinner does that." Before he could answer, she snapped her fingers together clumsily. "It's Suzy! She's the one with something in her oven and she's got gas." She thought she heard Jake choking when she added, "And she's horny all the time."

"That's um . . . tough," Jake said, still sounding wheezy.

"You bet your ass it is." She nodded. "I want to ride your big stick all the time too so I understand that. When we get home, I'm totally doing that to you. Just wait, it's going to be the hottest thing ever."

Patting her hand, Jake said, "I'm sure it will, baby."

They fell silent for the rest of the trip. At one point, Lydia thought she'd actually woken herself up snoring. She wasn't sure how that was possible since she didn't remember going to sleep. *Wow, what is Jake doing? Why is the truck rocking so much? Back and forth, back and forth.* "Honey," she said weakly. "I'm not feeling too good. Could you please keep the vehicle straight?"

"Oh shit," she heard him mutter.

One moment, she was sitting beside him on the way home, and the next, she was bent over a bush in the front yard as her two or maybe three margaritas staged a revolt. Through it all, Jake was right there with her. Holding her up and keeping her hair out of the way. He was her white knight and absolutely the one man she wanted around when she was tossing her cookies. In her drunken state, she had a startling moment of clarity. Real men—the keepers—weren't there just for the good times or the amazing sex. No, they were there beside you in the trenches when you were at your lowest and they still looked at you as if they were the luckiest bastards alive. Any guy can be a husband, but only a real man will ever use his shirt to wipe your face after you've defaced the magnolia bush in clear sight of all the neighbors at midnight. And that same man will carry you in the house, brush your teeth even though your breath smells worse than a dead cat, and then hold you up while he stands in the shower fully clothed himself to clean you off. He will dress your limp body and tuck you lovingly into bed, where he will stay awake to check on you repeatedly throughout the night.

As she felt him kiss her forehead and say, "I love you," Lydia knew that through all the heartache and loss in her life, she'd found it. The guy who had turned into a man just to love her. It wasn't that he was better than Brett had been. It was quite simply that when God took one angel from her life, he blessed her three years later with another one. Their beginning might have been unconventional, but in the end, they'd gotten it right, and wasn't that all any couple could hope for? Each love story takes a different route, but if you truly love each other, you'll always reach your destination together, no matter what road you travel to get there.

Epilogue

"I thought your wedding was the social event of the year," Lydia marveled as she stared at the setup for the sunset wedding on the private beach of the Oceanix–Myrtle Beach resort.

"Isn't this gorgeous," Crystal whispered in awe. "You have to give Mia credit. When she finally accepted Seth's marriage proposal, she jumped in with both feet."

"She's been like bridezilla from what I've heard." Gwen snickered as the three friends stood together waiting for the service to begin. The billowing white canopies and tents looked amazing against the setting sun as people slowly began to fill the chairs assembled in rows on the sand.

"Sweet man sandwich," Emma hissed as she carefully navigated the shifting surface in her heels. "Have you seen the Jackson brothers and cousins?"

"Okay, point them out, but be discreet," Lydia instructed, hoping that Jake wouldn't notice their fixation on the handsome resort owners.

Emma lowered her voice and said, "Do you see that woman wearing the hideous mustard yellow polyester dress?" When they all cringed but nodded, she continued, "Okay, look to the left of her and back near the first set of torches."

Crystal was the first to say, "Oh, yeah, I see them. Some of them were at our wedding, but I don't really remember much from that day."

"Sweet baby Jesus," Gwen groaned as her eyes widened. "They sure are hot. I bet they have manly names like Rutherford or Brick."

Emma giggled as she shook her head. "I'm not sure which name goes with whom, but you're looking at Rhett, Asher, Dylan, and Luke. Those are Seth's brothers. Now, the ones walking up on the other side are the cousins and they run resorts as well. I haven't managed to get their names but look at them. Who in the hell cares? You could call each of them Bubba and they'd still be total studs."

"You're talking about the Jacksons, aren't you?" Suzy Merimon laughed knowingly as she walked up. You would never know that she'd given birth to a daughter less than two months earlier. She'd regained her slim figure with an ease that would make most women hate her.

"You're damned right we are." Emma sighed. "I mean look at that man flesh. They're rich, sexy as hell, and standing like they've got ten-inch cocks."

"This is like a movie or television show," Beth groaned as she came striding over. "I swear they look too good to be real."

Before anyone could respond, Claire, Ava, and Ella came hurrying toward them, while darting glances over their shoulders. None too subtly, Ella nodded her head and said, "Did you see—"

"The Jacksons," they all said together before laughter filled the air.

"I know it's wrong," Claire whispered, "but look at them. What kind of gene pool must that family have?"

"They've got the best teeth," Crystal added, before shrugging when everyone stared at her. "What? They do. They're so perfectly straight and white. Just imagine what a shame it would be if they had buck teeth."

Ever loyal to her sister, Ella agreed. "That would be a tragedy. Although I'd think someone with their money could afford to make sure that never happens."

Just then, the wedding planner indicated that it was time for everyone to take their seats. Seth and Mia didn't have the traditional bridal party. They didn't feel right about excluding anyone, so they'd decided to forgo that altogether. Since it was one of their own getting married, the ladies had arranged to sit together ahead of time with their husbands taking the row behind them.

Claire, Suzy, Beth, Ella, Emma, Gwen, Ava, Crystal, and Lydia joined hands as Mia made her way down the aisle holding the arm of her mother and her father to the song "Thinking Out Loud," by Ed Sheeran. Her simple sleeveless white dress floated behind her across the sand, reminding Lydia of a fairy princess.

Seth stood under an arbor woven with lilies and white silk. He had eyes only for his bride as she kissed her parents and skipped the rest of the way to his side. Their vows were simple and heartfelt, and within moments, they were kissing each other and the officiant was proclaiming them Mr. and Mrs. Seth Jackson. As Mia reached their aisle with her new husband, she stopped and hugged each of her friends. Before she pulled away, she whispered, "Did you get a load of the rest of his family?" Before anyone could answer, she'd given them an impish grin and turned to embrace Seth.

The men descended on them then to claim their women and they all entered the huge tents where the reception was being held. Lydia found a quiet corner and motioned Jake toward it. They hadn't been alone together in hours, and as always, she'd missed him. "Hey, baby," he said softly before kissing her lightly on the lips. "I can't wait to get out of here later so I can have some alone time with my wife."

Lydia nodded eagerly in response. As usual, they were on the same page. "Mia said that they plan to leave in the next hour or so. We'll be right on their heels." Leaning her head against his shoulder, she added, "This has been such a magical night, hasn't it?"

Looking at her intently, Jake asked, "Sweetheart, do you want a big wedding? I've told you several times that I'd be happy for us to do that. I know a wedding in Vegas isn't exactly every woman's dream. Just say the word and it's yours."

Giving a sigh of contentment, she shook her head. "It may have been different than I'd always thought it would be, but I don't care. There's no way I'm going back and rewriting history. That's when we were married. We spent that first night together then—well, kind of—and you put this ring on my finger," she added, wiggling the sparkling diamond. "I don't want a do-over because I'm blissfully happy with my life as it is." That was such an understatement, she thought. Being Jake's wife and Casey's stepmother felt as natural to her as breathing. Jake had been granted joint custody of his daughter just a few weeks earlier, and she knew that he was relieved to have the whole thing behind him. Chris hadn't attempted to block him in the end. Lydia felt sure it had more to do with possibly missing his generous support than not wanting to subject her daughter to an ugly court battle. After all, Chris continued to be—well, Chris. Thankfully, she was dating someone now, and even though she was rarely friendly to Lydia, she seemed to be too occupied with her new boyfriend to expend as much time on unpleasantness. God help them all if she was dumped.

"I love you," Jake murmured then pulled her from her chair and tucked her on his lap.

Lydia knew she should be embarrassed that they were carrying on like teenagers, but looking around the room, she discovered that they were far from alone. Jason Danvers stood slowly dancing in place with his wife, Claire, in his arms. You didn't need to hear the words because the love between them was obvious for all to see. A few feet away, Gray Merimon's eyes were riveted on his wife, Suzy, as she spoke to another couple. Every few seconds, Gray's hand would stroke lovingly up and down her spine and she'd get the softest smile on her face. Then there was Nick Merimon, curled around his wife and whispering something in her ear. Lydia could see the blush steal over Beth's cheeks as she cuddled closer to her husband.

Curious as to where the rest of their friends were, Lydia looked around the room until she located Declan Stone sitting beside his wife, Ella. They were talking softly to each other as Declan twirled a strand of her hair around his finger. He laughed at something she said before leaning forward to drop a kiss onto the tip of her nose. Next, there was Mac Powers with his arm around his wife, Ava's waist while they spoke to Ava's brother, Brant, and his fiancée, Emma. Lydia wondered if the women knew that even as their men spoke to each other, their eyes never left the woman at their side. At one point, Mac rubbed Ava's stomach, and Lydia had to wonder if there would be an announcement coming from them soon. And Emma lit up like the Fourth of July when Brant caressed her cheek with his finger. Just a few feet away stood Gwen and Dominic. They'd finally informed all of their friends and family that they'd been married for some time now. When Gwen stood on her tiptoes to throw her arms around Dominic's neck and hug him close, he obliged her by bending lower and gently encircling her waist before straightening and lifting her off her feet. The honeymoon obviously wasn't over for those two.

"What are you looking at?" Jake asked as he glanced around, trying to see what had her attention.

"Wait just a second," she requested as she attempted to locate her last two friends. Ah, there was Mark

DeSanto laughing with his cousin, Denny, while keeping Crystal locked firmly against his side. Lydia couldn't miss the possessiveness in his touch as he hooked a hand around the nape of her neck to keep her from straying. The heat they generated between them with just one look was enough to power the city for a month.

And finally, there were the newlyweds, Mia and Seth. Mia had once said that Seth was a traditional man who wanted to build a home and a family with her once she was ready to settle down. Lydia didn't think Seth could possibly have any doubts that he and his bride had finally arrived at the same place. Mia hadn't taken her eyes off him since Lydia had been watching, and likewise, his beautiful bride equally captivated Seth. Lydia had to giggle, though, when in true Mia fashion, she had her hand on her groom's ass while he spoke with his gorgeous relatives. Despite all of her teasing, it was obvious that Seth was the only Jackson that Mia would ever truly see.

As Jake helped her to her feet, Lydia paused once more to look around the tent to savor the sight of all of her blissful friends—the women of Danvers with the men they loved. In a resort town such as Myrtle Beach where anything seemed possible, Lydia wondered if there had ever been any doubt that they'd all get their happy ending.

The funny thing, though, was that the men in their lives were only a part of it. The one constant that each of them could fall back on again and again through the years would be their sisterhood. Ten women from different backgrounds who'd found each other at Danvers International, and no matter what life brought their way, that was a bond that would never unravel or break. And Lydia was so excited to step forward with these women at her side to see what the future would hold for them.

Continue reading for a special preview
of the new contemporary romance from
bestselling author Sydney Landon, which will
be coming from Berkley in Summer 2017!

Chapter One

Zoe Hart walked through the familiar lobby of the Oceanix Resort in Pensacola, Florida, but she saw none of its usual elegance and grandeur. She'd woken in a bad mood that morning, which was unusual since she normally loved her birthday. She was twenty-nine today and despite her best attempts, she was no closer to seducing her best friend, Dylan Jackson, than she had been last year. The situation wasn't helped by the fact that he was her landlord as well. She owned and operated the coffee shop in the Oceanix, Zoe's Place. Even though she worked her ass off to make it a success, she was so grateful to Dylan for giving her a chance when she was trying to get her business off the ground. All of the big coffee chains had vied to open a location in the ultra high-end resort, but Dylan had believed in her business plan and had celebrated her success every step of the way.

Her close friend and shop manager, Dana Anders, was busy loading the pastry display cases for another busy breakfast rush when Zoe arrived. The comforting smell of freshly brewed gourmet coffee filled the air and her stomach growled in response. For the first time that morning, she literally took a moment to stop and appreciate her surroundings. She'd designed the interior layout with comfort in mind, but had also wanted a place that appealed to a variety of customers. There were tables for her business customers who wanted to work while they drank their espressos. There were sofas for those who were truly enjoying their vacations and looking only to relax while they sipped frappes, and there were overstuffed chairs arranged in cozy seating areas for the groups who were recharging with a latte after a long day at the office or relishing a morning away from the kids. Of course with their location inside the hotel, they had people who came and went never to return. But she was particularly proud of the loyal local customers who had become like her friends and family.

"Well, well," Dana murmured as she noticed Zoe's dejected expression. "The birthday girl doesn't seem to be in the mood to celebrate this morning." Her friend patted the counter and sat down on a stool behind it. "Park it right there and tell me all about it." Before Zoe could open her mouth, Dana said, "No—no, let me take a guess. You're twenty-nine, still carrying around your big V-card and you've been friend-zoned by the man you've secretly lusted after for years. Wait! Actually, friend-zoned would be easier to deal with. Some friends have sex together all the time. You've been sister-zoned and that's the kiss of death if you're hoping for a fling."

Zoe planted her hands on the counter and shook her head vehemently. "I haven't been sister-zoned. I'm still completely and totally in the friend area. Dylan and I are buddies. We talk about all kinds of things you wouldn't discuss with your sibling."

Dana clucked her tongue before taking a big drink of the coffee she had sitting nearby. Finally, as if she were talking to a toddler she said, "Sweetie, when he hangs out with you, does he take calls and texts from other women?"

"Of course." Zoe ground her teeth, thinking of how much she hated overhearing any time he employed his sexy laugh on some bimbo of the month.

Putting a hand under her chin, Dana studied her for a moment before asking, "Does he ever tell you anything about his dates? As in bedroom stuff or kink level?"

"Yes, all the time," Zoe growled. "I guess that proves that he doesn't see me as his sister though, right?"

"It's worse than I thought," Dana said dramatically. "You're officially one of the guys. You've ceased to have a vagina where he's concerned."

"*WHAT?* No way!" Zoe sputtered. Pointing to her ample chest, she argued, "How could he miss these babies?"

Refusing to back down, Dana fired off, "Does he ever bump you on the shoulder with his fist? Or high-five you?"

Zoe's mouth went dry and she stared at Dana in growing horror before dropping her head onto the counter. "Oh God, I'm just like one of his guy friends," Zoe mumbled in despair. "You're absolutely right. I might as well have a penis."

Dana patted the top of her head consolingly. "I don't know about the whole having a dick thing. I'd say you're more gender neutral where he's concerned."

"Wow, that's so much better," she snapped. Dana was silent for so long, Zoe finally lifted her head, thinking maybe they'd had a customer wander in before the shop officially opened. Instead, her friend was giving her a calculating look that immediately made her nervous. "What?" she asked warily, not even sure she wanted to know what was running through the other woman's mind. She and Dana were about as opposite as two people could be, but regardless of that their friendship worked. Dana loved men in all shapes and sizes and seemed to be dating a new guy every week. She was adventurous, outgoing, and the customers absolutely adored her. She stood just over five feet tall with short blond hair and a personality that made everyone feel special. A few years back, not long after Zoe had hired her, Dana had convinced her to come out for a drink. Zoe had ended up having several past her limit and had drunkenly admitted to Dana that she'd had a crush on Dylan for years. She'd also confessed to being a virgin, something that had blown the other woman away. After that, Dana had tried her best to set Zoe up on blind dates, but none of them compared to the infatuation she carried where Dylan was concerned. The heart wanted what it wanted—and Zoe's appeared to be particularly stubborn.

Dana folded her arms and leaned forward. "You can come back from this. As long as you haven't entered the death zone where he looks at you like his little sister, there's always hope. We can turn this around . . . *if* you'll really apply yourself. Starting with that." Dana pointed to Zoe's white polo shirt as she spoke.

Zoe frowned, looking down in confusion. "What's wrong with my clothes?"

"Sweetie, if you want Dylan to stop seeing you as a member of his dude squad, then you can't continue to dress like one of the guys." When Zoe opened her mouth to protest, Dana held her hand up. "What are they wearing when they come in here for coffee before hitting the golf course?"

"I've never noticed . . ." Zoe began before Dana interrupted her.

"Cut the crap," Dana huffed, "you know they dress just like that. Polo shirts and khaki shorts. Dylan sees you as one of the guys because you blend in so well with them. It's time for that to stop. You have so much going for you. Big tits, small waist, and plenty of butt. You need to dress to showcase your assets." As Zoe gulped, Dana pointed to her hair. "And that spinster bun has got to go. Your hair is gorgeous, but I've only seen you wear it down a few times and that was when I hid those freaking bands that you seem to have a million of. Men go crazy over long, wavy hair, which you naturally possess. You don't need a lot of makeup because you look great without it. Let's just start with the things that I've mentioned and I guarantee that in no time, Dylan will be tripping over his tongue."

"I don't know . . ." Zoe murmured. "Clothes really don't change anything. I'm still the same person that he's known for years. I could probably parade around naked in front of him and it wouldn't make a difference. It seems silly to pretend to be someone I'm not."

Dana walked around the counter and put an arm around her. "Honey, men are visual creatures. You and Dylan have been friends since you were children. He's grown up thinking of you in a certain way. We're just attempting to show him that there is another side he's never seen before. He's overlooking the fact that you're a beautiful woman who is flipping perfect for him. Right or wrong, sometimes a new set of curtains makes the room look completely different."

A giggle burst from her lips and Zoe grinned at Dana. "Are you comparing me to draperies now?"

"Hey, I'm just trying to give you something to work with. Now go ahead and tell me you're on board. No, let's go one better than that." Dana pulled far enough away to extend a hand to her. "Zoe. Do you agree to do whatever it takes to finally land the man of your dreams this year? Are you prepared to surrender that v-card to Dylan before your thirtieth birthday? If so, let's shake on it. No wimping out though. We're declaring war on the friend-zone with Dylan. Are you ready to trade in your polos for plunging necklines and rising hemlines? Once you agree, there's no going back."

As Dana wiggled her hand impatiently, Zoe thought back over the revelations her friend had just waved at her feet. Could it really be that simple? Had Dylan overlooked the fact that she was a potential romantic partner because she'd never made the effort to show off her feminity? And truthfully, she knew that she dressed for comfort most days. Her mother, who'd been the executive chef at the Oceanix for years, rarely wore makeup or fancy outfits, so Zoe hadn't grown up wearing dresses or bows in her hair. She'd been a tomboy and possibly she'd never stopped seeing herself that way. But now she was almost thirty and she couldn't keep pining away for a man who didn't want her.

She'd let Dana help her and spend this next year giving it everything she had. If at the end, she and Dylan were still only friends, then she'd have to accept that and move on with her life. As much as she cared for him, she wanted a husband and children of her own at some point in the future.

So, straightening her spine, Zoe took Dana's hand and gave it an enthusiastic shake. "Let's do this," she said bravely. *Please let Dylan be the one*, she thought to herself as she listened to Dana's plans for their first steps. The next twelve months might not go as Zoe wanted, but they certainly wouldn't be boring.

Chapter Two

It had been a hell of a long week and Dylan Jackson was looking forward to kicking back and relaxing. He usually had dinner with Zoe at least one evening a week, but thanks to a business trip to one of the other Oceanix Resorts, it had been closer to two since he'd seen her last and he missed her. He'd even missed her birthday, which he tried never to do. He'd texted her earlier and she'd suggested they meet in one of the resort restaurants since neither of them had felt like cooking. Dylan lived in the penthouse so it was a simple matter for him to take the elevator back downstairs at seven. He'd figured Zoe was working late at the coffee shop as she usually did, but when she responded to his text she'd already been at her condominium a few miles away from the hotel.

He walked into the restaurant and automatically headed for his usual reserved table in the corner. It was both private and had an amazing view of the gulf. He'd been so busy looking around that he was abruptly brought up short when he realized that his table was occupied. A woman with long, dark hair cascading down her back sat in one of the chairs sipping a glass of wine. Dylan stifled a surge of irritation. Even though the woman looked stunning from behind, now he'd have to deal with the aggravation of either asking her to move or finding somewhere else to sit himself, which would be no small feat as the restaurant was packed.

As he stood uncertainly pondering his options, the woman turned, seemingly sensing him behind her and he froze. He blinked a few times thinking he was imagining things. Then she smiled and it hit him with the force of a sledgehammer. "What are you waiting for, an engraved invitation?" She laughed as she motioned him closer.

Dear God, what was going on here? The woman with the short, clingy dress, amazing legs, and plump breasts sounded like his best friend. If he looked closely, her features were the same. But everything else was wrong—very wrong. Zoe wore her hair in a ponytail and dressed in sensible clothing. Half the time she had a coffee stain on her white polo. She didn't make his mouth go dry—or his cock go hard. She was his buddy, the one constant in his life that never changed.

"Did someone die?" he finally asked, thinking maybe she'd been to a funeral or something. Why else would she be wearing a dress?

She wrinkled her nose, as she was prone to do when she was thinking before shaking her head. "Er . . . no." Giving him a look of concern, she reached out and put a hand on his arm. "Are you alright? You look rather pale. Would you rather we just go upstairs to your place and order in? I'm fine with that if you're tired."

"NO!" He protested loudly, causing people at nearby tables to look over at him. Great, he was making an ass out of himself. But there was no way he was going somewhere more private with Zoe looking like . . . that. He needed to get to the bottom of this, preferably in public with lots of people around. So, he took a breath and made an effort to collect himself. He stepped forward and took his seat. He was saved from making conversation while they placed their orders, but after the waiter had gone, an unusually awkward silence settled between them.

This type of thing never happened between them and he found he wasn't sure how to handle it. Should he go ahead and ask her why she looked the way she did? Or ignore it and hope it never happened again?

She moved closer to him, putting her new and improved breasts only inches from his hand. "You seem a little stressed out," she said softly. "Are you sure you're okay?"

To his utter horror, he heard himself blurting out, "What's happened to you?" He pointed to her outfit, and then quickly gulped down a drink of his water. Maybe he was getting sick. His throat was so parched.

"What are you talking about?" she asked, looking at him as if he'd lost his mind. Hell, he was beginning to think she was right. He needed to look into his family's health history a little closer.

He knew he sounded nuts, but he couldn't stop

himself from saying, "The dress, and the hair. You're even wearing high heels. You know those make your feet hurt."

"Oh, I've got a date later," Zoe shrugged. She gave him a bright smile, and then began filling him in on what he'd missed at the resort while he was away. She appeared to have no clue that he wasn't an active participant in the conversation. Making small talk seemed impossible for him right now because all he wanted to do was demand to know who she was going out with. He'd figured they'd watch a movie after dinner as they normally did, but apparently that wasn't going to happen. Dylan had never been one for change and this transformation was almost more than he could wrap his head around. He knew Zoe though. This was just a one-time thing. She'd go back to looking the way she usually did tomorrow and then his world would be back in balance once again. Otherwise, he was going to have to face the fact that somewhere along the way his best friend had turned into a very desirable woman. And that he was afraid could only spell disaster for the relationship that he'd always valued above all others in his life.

Sydney Landon is the *New York Times* and *USA Today* bestselling author of the Danvers Novels, including *The One for Me*, *Watch Over Me*, *Always Loving You*, and *No Denying You*. She lives in South Carolina with her husband and two children, who keep life interesting and borderline insane, but never boring. When she isn't writing, Sydney enjoys reading, swimming, and being a minivan-driving soccer mom. Visit her online at sydneylandon.com, facebook.com/sydney.landonauthor, and twitter.com/SydneyLandon1.

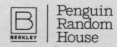